CW00411265

Lupa

Marie Marshall

P'kaboo Publishers
South Africa
2012

P'kaboo Publishers
www.pkaboo.net

First Edition
2012

Copyright © Licensed to:
P'kaboo Publishers
South Africa

Cover design: Aludar8

ISBN 978-0-9870103-5-3

~ Lupa ~

Acknowledgements:

Lucy P. Naylor who told me to write this book; and my literary agents, Bookseeker Agency in Perth.

~

"Quis iniquae tam patiens urbis."

CHAPTER I

"I'm a Serb – and no, that isn't an apology! People don't want to hear about atrocities *to* Serbs, and that's fine by me, because I don't want to talk about the subject!"

"I wasn't going to ask," said Vittorio.

"That's fine then!"

Undoubtedly this marks a low point in our relationship, and as it happened during our first ever conversation, it sometimes surprises me that we ever got any further with each other. I put the fact that we did down to a base motive on my own part.

It had been one of those days. I was stiff and aching anyway, and my temper was worsened by having been caught in a rain shower, and having had to leap for my life as I tried to cross the road. The traffic in Rome can be bloody, and the prickly feeling under my armpits at an escape from being a statistic was made worse by having to endure a spray of filthy water over my legs and a spray of filthier language from the driver who had nearly mown me down.

So I was in no mood for bother of any sort when I took refuge in a café, searched my bag and pockets for coins, and ordered a cappuccino. Bother came. Being fairly flustered I lost a grip of my best Italian, and tripped over a bit of grammar which had given me problems since the time I first tried to learn the language in school. The man behind the bar didn't react at all, but the person standing behind me corrected me by quietly repeating the phrase I had used, but with the solecism edited. I was blazing, I turned round and told him what I thought of his effrontery, and here's where the base motive comes into it – my remonstrance sort of tailed off because, frankly, he was attractive. Frankly, he was very attractive.

"I am sorry. I deserve that. It was rude of me," he said. "Let me get these coffees, it's the least I can do. I insist."

This was laughable – old fashioned – but my objection to such patronising behaviour seemed to die in my throat before I could say anything. I just thought it. How dare he insult me and then think he could buy me off with a cappuccino and some superficial Roman charm. But nevertheless, I allowed myself to be ushered to a seat, which was held for me to sit down, and to be brought my drink. More, I allowed him to hang my jacket carefully over a spare chair, and accepted the loan of his handkerchief to dry some of the muck from my legs.

Who carries a handkerchief these days?

Part of me felt like kicking his shins, but perhaps I was more angry at myself than at him, because I could not see anything in his face or demeanour to suggest that he was other than genuinely sorry for his rudeness and genuinely determined to make up for it. Why more angry at myself? I told you, he was very good-looking. He was perhaps about twenty years older than me, but no more than that - tall, slim, and in a tailored, midnight-blue suit which looked bespoke, rather than off-the-peg. His hair was dark, had a wave in it, and was cut in a fairly young style, as if he were the new manager of Lazio, or intended to run for mayor of Milan. No, there was more class about it than that, and it looked natural, as if it had simply grown that way when he was a boy, and had stayed that way. His eyes were blue, like Terence Hill's (I watch a lot of spaghetti westerns these days). He had an air of *insouciance* which over the course of our conversation, quite against my will, gradually put me at my ease. I don't usually go for men in their forties, and I won't say that I had suddenly gone weak-kneed and gooey about this one, but I found myself feeling more flattered than I ought to be, if you see what I mean. That's why. Women just don't do this sort of thing any more, we like to tell ourselves.

As I recall, I stared blankly over my coffee-cup and out of the window – which makes it strange that I should now be able to describe him. Perhaps I looked him up and down later. No, I remember how he got my attention.

He did most of the talking. He introduced himself, said he had some semi-official position – part archaeologist, part diplomat, or so it sounded. "Oh yeah," I thought to myself. "Good story, good chat-up line." Anyhow, he said he had "connections" here and there, but was currently supervising a student "dig" here in the city. The city. That's how he said it – "*La Città*", as if it had quotation marks around it. I suddenly realised that he was a little embarrassed, and was groping for things to say, hoping to unfreeze my mood. His *insouciance* was slipping somewhat, but that minor change was – oh good grief – rather endearing.

"My friends call me Vittorio. Please feel free to do the same," he said.

Why? I thought. I'm never going to see you again, and I'm going back to the flat as soon as I've drunk this coffee!

Suddenly: "I know who you are. You're *L'Amazonina*." That got my attention! That's when I looked him up and down.

"I haven't gone by that name for two years. I guess I ought to be pleased someone still recognises me. I haven't worked in the circus since I had my fall."

"Is that where you got that scar?" he said. That total disregard of tact! How did he square his antique charm with blunt rudeness? My hand flew automatically to my forehead to cover up what was only a little blemish which, for most of the time, I managed to forget.

"I'm sorry." Another apology.

"It's nothing," I lied. "I'm told the horse kicked out when I fell, and just caught me with a hoof. I can't remember much about it, but I haven't worked as a bareback rider since."

"Your accent – it's Balkan." Blunt again. That's where my mouthful of Serbian angst came from. Then of course, after an awkward silence, it was my turn to apologise.

"My real name is Jelena Stepanović," I said, and we shook hands. Things got better. Outside it had stopped raining. I was dry and when I looked down I could not see much evidence of the spray on my shoes or skirt. He told me to keep the handkerchief. Up to now I had retained an obstinate knot between my shoulder blades, but it was time to relax and let it go. He wasn't bad company when all was said and done, and we chatted a little more about his archaeological interests. I tried to remember the last time I was at ease in a man's company, and couldn't. Since Franjo, since all the things that had happened to me back home, since coming to Italy and working in a strange circus, I had always kept my guard up. Vittorio, it seemed, had got in behind it, but having done so he did not press on. I found myself trying to figure out how bluntness of speech, obvious charm, and great reserve managed to sit so well in one man, and how they made him complete.

Our first conversation was not deep, and now I come to think about it none of them were. Other things that we came to share were more profound, things that we experienced together without much in the way of words – but I'm running ahead. Let me try and tell this one chapter at a time, much as it did, in fact, unfold.

No, it was not deep, but neither was it small talk. It was the casual rap of two reasonably intelligent people, I thought. Eventually a lull coincided with the dregs of my cappuccino cooling beyond the point where they were pleasant to drink, and I made to stand up. He was up first, pulling back my seat for me, and offering to help me on with my jacket. As a gesture of independence, I reached for it with one hand, and put it on unassisted. We stepped into the street together.

"Do you live far from here? May I walk you there?"

"Via Stoccolma, not far from the Velodrome – I'm flat-sitting for some friends who are out of the country. And yes, at least I'd welcome company part of the way," I said, trying to insist on our regarding ourselves as equals, not as protector and protégée. We walked, side by side, and he casually slid one hand into his trouser pocket as if to show that he too had relaxed, that he too was comfortable and accepted at least a show of equality. As days went by, and I got to know him better, I too began to be comfortable with his chivalrous little mannerisms, although they could never entirely be shaken loose from a slight air of assumed seniority. We were – I told myself – equal but different; after all, *he* would never be able to do hand-stands on a horse! It was at least half an hour's walk, and in other circumstances I might have taken the underground. He did not insist on seeing me right to my door. Rather, when I determinedly stopped with a street to cross and a hundred and fifty metres or so still to walk, and offered him my hand, he shook it firmly and held it for less than a moment.

"Well, goodbye," I said, and turned to go.

"Come and see the dig tomorrow, if you're free," he said suddenly, checking me as I was about to go for a gap in the traffic. I stopped, the gap filled, my determination to go on with my life wavered, and I felt a little frisson of guilty relief.

I agreed, and found myself giving him my telephone number. We shook hands again, and with a "Ciao!" I found another serendipitous gap in the traffic. I dived for it, and used the increasing distance between him and me to hide the fact that a blush had sprung into my cheek. A few strides down the pavement on the far side of the street, and I had begun to convince myself that I was angry at myself again. But try as I might, I couldn't resist the temptation to look over my shoulder. In fact I stopped and watched until he was out of sight. *He* didn't look back once.

When I was back at the flat, I took stock. It occurred to me – and now I come to think about it, this is something that I want you all to remember – that nothing is ever quite what it seems. Least of all things that we thought were permanent. There is no such thing as permanence. Everything is superficial, and the truth, if it is anywhere, is underneath. Sometimes it isn't even there.

When I was a little girl, everything seemed to be just so. I was one of Tito's children, as well as my parents'. We had always been a circus family, and had moved about Yugoslavia with an ease which surprises my friends in the West when I explain it to them. But Yugoslavia was like that. And Tito seemed to be immortal, just like Mao or Castro in their countries, just like Franco and Salazar had been in theirs. There would always be Communism, and somewhere else in the world there would always be Apartheid – that was simply the way the world was. The fact that once upon a time these things had been new, not old, did not occur to me. I don't believe it occurred to anyone.

Our home was in Srebrenice, at least that was our *pied-a-terre* when we were not touring with the circus; I was a Serb child of Serbian parents and, although I had travelled from Skopje to Ljubljana and back, I had never actually lived in Serbia. I never asked "what" my friends were, but only considered that they were my friends. It mattered little to me that some of them had different accents, or had Friday off, or that on Sundays some of them came out of their front door and turned right, while others came out and turned left. Life was just this way. I imitated their accents, I peeked in through a window of the mosque, we taught each other the various liturgies our old folk used and played games with them – I found that enormous fun and a little rebellious, as my parents were good Communists, didn't go to church, and didn't even consider sending me.

The day after Tito died it seemed to me, in my youth, that everything just went on as it did. Only later did I come to realise that everything *had* changed, that it would never be the same again, it was all completely different. All that had happened, when I first realised this, was that the Federal army had moved into Slovenia. But suddenly it was as if I didn't recognise the world outside any more. Even at home there was a different atmosphere. Nothing was said, but some of the laughter died, and I saw something in my mother and father's eyes which I can only suppose, now I come to think about it, must have been fear.

Truths were no longer truths. Tito, said one person or another, had tricked the allies during World War 2 into supporting him in a civil war. Tito, said another person again, though a Croat had built up a Serbian empire. People who basically spoke the same language, and who had lived peacefully next door to each other for years, began to look askance at each other. People's conversations now contained generalisations – all Croats are so-and-so, all Muslims are such-and-such. But what about Milos or Marian? Oh they're different, they're my friends. Until one day they weren't any longer.

Franjo was my boyfriend. His family were from Dubrovnik, but he had been studying in Srebrenice, and had eventually got a job there. I thought no more about his ethnicity than he did about mine. It was not even part of our vocabulary. Do you know what? It was better that way. Yes, disagree with me if you like, despise me if you must, but the way things were when I was a girl were better, more solid. You knew where you were. At least *I* knew where *I* was. Franjo and I might have got married eventually. I liked him very much, and we sometimes talked about the future. But by and large we were simply easy in each other's company and in each other's arms, and felt that was enough for now. But there came a day when even his eyes began to look different. We didn't talk about our differences, but we could hear other people doing so. I once saw him talking to a group of men in a café; I was going to cross the street and join them, but something stopped me, something about the men seemed dangerous, although they were, to all intents, ordinary. Another time, whilst waiting for him by a bus stop, I saw him waylaid by a knot of people. They were about a hundred and fifty meters away from me, and I couldn't see them well, but they could have been the men from the café. Franjo had seemed to be arguing with them, and had a worried look on his face when eventually he reached me.

Then one day he wasn't there. The rumour was that he had gone to join a Croat militia. I knew he would not have gone willingly, as he was a gentle boy, but perhaps the men I saw him with knew where his family lived in Dubrovnik. I had to accept that I would never see him again.

The speed of change from that day! I couldn't speak or write of how my parents died, or of how I came to Italy – I meant what I said to Vittorio. No, I could only say change, change, and change again, nothing the same from one day to the next, nothing permanent. In Italy I found circus work again, and a little fame as *L'Amazonina*, but only for a while. I no longer expected permanence, you see. So in a funny way I was not surprised when my accident happened, and put me out of the circus. Suddenly without work, I didn't even know whether I was in Italy legally. I was living on the savings from my circus work, in a flat that wasn't my own, I hardly knew who I was or where I was.

Sometimes, when I felt as though I had nothing better to do, I sat at the window, or leant precariously against it with my head making a greasy mark I would later have to wipe off, and looked out, down towards the end of the street, at what I could see of *la Città*.

If it was the morning after a night I had been lying awake with thoughts of insurmountable problems chasing round my brain (only to fade to nothing when I eventually got up) or a night when my dreams were all vague stress, travelling, or sitting in meetings where I had no idea what was going on, then I felt that what I was looking at was just not real.

It was two-dimensional, a series of rapidly changing two-dimensional scenes, no more solid or substantial than the collection of fascist postcards in the albums on my friend's shelves. Or that it was all like an onion, with skin after skin to peel away, and then with very little, or nothing, left at the centre. At night, the lights outside were not attached to anything, they just existed as lights, static or moving. More than once I came to with a jerk, and realised that I had fallen asleep as I stood with my head against the window. Sometimes I felt utterly exhausted, sometimes I felt as if the weight of impermanence would drive me mad.

CHAPTER II

It is late afternoon. I have reached the barracks, almost too late to do business. My arrival at this hour is deliberate, as if, despite it all, I want to leave myself some sort of get-out, an excuse to say, "It's too late, I'll come back tomorrow or next week." Or not at all.

In front of me is the iron gateway, securely locked, and the high, grey wall. I have seen it once before when I passed down this street on I don't know what errand, but without really paying that much attention. And now I can't remember what that errand was – the irrelevant search for it comes into my mind, as if another excuse to go no further – what could I have possibly wanted in this part of town anyway? I see and notice, now possibly for the first time, that there is a smaller doorway to the right of the gate, and that a couple of thugs are lounging there, doing their best to turn their guard-duty into a kind of stationary swagger. That's the best I can describe it. They don't see me, or if they do they pay little attention. The barracks gets its share of regular gawpers, especially women, or so I've heard.

I can see through the gate to the yard behind. It is empty at the moment, and half in shadow as the sun is low. Across the yard is the barracks itself, a single storey building much lower than the wall around it. Now I am aware that the sounds of Rome are becoming muted, to the extent that the screeching of swallows as they dart from eaves to eaves is more noticeable, as I stand here with my hands on my hips, watching them. Another diversion. Watch us, don't go through with this.

Now one of the thugs at the doorway is looking at me. The look is without expression, but to me it is a challenge, and the swallows and any other possible diversion at this moment becomes irrelevant. Only my bloody-mindedness matters. So I square my shoulders and walk across the street.

Rubicon number one.

I am heading straight for the doorway. The bully-boy who has noticed me mutters something to his mate, and now they are both looking at me. They are no longer lounging, they are standing in my way. Again it crosses my mind that this would a perfectly understandable excuse for turning round and going home. Home. Now, there's a word to play with!

"Can I help you, miss?" The enquiry is barely polite, almost dismissive.

"No, but the boss can," I reply. "I want to see him." The two look at each other, and there is a hint of amusement or even contempt in that look, which makes me grit my teeth. Damn it, I will get through that door despite them!

"Do you have an appointment?" Not even polite this time.

"I'll see him without one," I say. "Now. See to it, please." Actually I'm perspiring. I'm standing here facing down two toughs, each with more height, weight and reach than I have, and the only things fuelling my courage are plain awkwardness and the fact that I am tired of being messed about. I guess they are too, and they have their orders not to put up with persistent nuisances, fans, and troublemakers; that's why one of them lunges to grab me. He gets me side on, and I barge us both into the door jamb, which knocks a bit of wind out of him. The other is slower to react, which gives me enough time to kick him in the stomach. The first fellow's collision with the masonry has allowed me to free my left arm enough to get out the knife I carry in my waist-band, and to give him a shallow but deliberate cut across the back of his wrist. He gives a hiss, and lets me go.

I step back a couple of paces, narrowing the angle between them and adopting an easy stance with three fifths of my weight on my back leg, and holding my knife to the right – underhand grip – ready for either a wide slash or a short jab. I don't know how this is going to turn out. I hadn't imagined any of this when I resolved to come here. I don't want to die here in the street, as they probably have blades hidden somewhere too. They are standing there, thinking about the right way to pounce, it seems. But the pause we are suddenly in seems to make all three of us relax, just a little.

"Come on, boys. It's late in the working day. We don't want to be doing this. Take me to the boss. I'll say 'Please'."

The fellow whose wrist I cut claps his good hand over the wound, and says to his mate, "Get the lady a stool. I'll go and see if himself is free," and off through the doorway he goes, whilst the other one reaches inside and brings out a camp-stool. With a raised eyebrow, he affects a slight bow, and motions me to the stool. I step over, put one foot upon it, and rest my forearms on my knee. An unladylike pose, but I am not feeling like a lady. We watch each other for about five minutes, and then the first one comes back, wrapping a bandage round his hand.

"He's coming down."

I shake my head. "I'm going up. Show me the way." With no more objection than a shrug, he turns about and walks back the way he came. I step through the doorway and follow him. Behind me, his mate shuts the door and remains out in the street.

Rubicon number two, and I hardly notice it's being crossed!

The sand in the yard is hot underfoot, and well-trampled by bare feet and sandaled. There is a line, made by the shadow of the barrack roof, where the sand turns black, and no footprints are visible, but I imagine they are there nevertheless, and that either moonlight or the next morning's sun will reveal them, hinting at the business of the previous day, until the new day's traffic obliterates them with fresh prints.

It is cooler in the shadows, and my sweat is not quite dry and makes me shiver. Steady! They may take it for nerves. And now I look ahead to another doorway, this time in the barrack building itself. Above the doorway is something I have not seen, or not noticed, from outside. There is a small second storey, big enough to contain a couple of rooms, like a watch tower in a fort perhaps. There is one window in the upper storey, and we are being watched from it. We go in through this second doorway, and we are at the foot of some stairs, where the bully-boy stops and stands aside for me. I look up the stairs, straight into the face of the boss, who is standing at the top, as if he was about to come down.

"This must be urgent," he says. I search for sarcasm, but find none and give up the search in favour of appraising him.

I don't know what I am expecting to see. Well, that's not quite true, because I have been trying to shake two images from my mind. The first was of a fawning, Syrian merchant in brocades and jewellery, dancing attendance on patrician patrons and wheedling the manager of the arena for a better cut. As I was being led across the yard, this was replaced briefly by the idea of someone bigger than his bruisers – a veteran of the ring, with a scarred face. Both of these are surely too melodramatic! Anyhow, now I look at him, the boss, the *Lanista*, I do not know whether to be impressed, surprised, or disappointed.

This is the king of this little country-within-Rome, who rules a large squad of professional fighters with a handful of heavies, and he looks quite ordinary. No jewels and brocades, no great muscles, no scars. Well-proportioned and fit enough, but with the air of someone who does not have to fight, he would be pleasant-faced if he bothered to smile. He is clean-shaven and close-cropped, and wears nothing more flamboyant than a *toga virilis*. "Come up," he says, and I obey the king, as one does. Bully-boy, nursing his hand a little more overtly to show the king how he has suffered in his service, follows me up.

Up the stairs is a spartan office – a table, a couple of chairs, some shelves with manuscripts stacked on them, another with a few household gods, these are the only furnishings. There is a wide window, out of which I steal a glance; it looks out into the barracks ring. Someone is gathering up equipment, and stowing it with a clatter, just out of my field of vision. In one wall of the room is an opening which must lead into another room, but it is curtained off. Suddenly I am aware again of the racket of the swallows. They must be nesting beneath the pantiles, outside the window.

"I was about to go home. Business hours are over," he says, quietly, as we stand facing each other. "But I gather from the assault you made upon my employees that this is a matter that won't wait. I am not a patient man at times like these, and my dinner is waiting. But in deference to one who is obviously a person of family, I have not sent for the city watch, but have decided to receive you. Now, what is your urgent business?"

I understand. This is where the real fight takes place. The kick-and-stab show with the two gatekeepers was just a bit of shadow-boxing. Am I up to this? Am I going home tonight with my cheeks burning?

"I want to train here."

"I do not give private lessons. You have wasted your time."

"Do I come on like someone who wants to pay for a few private lessons?"

"I can't say what you come on like. If it comes to that, my squad gets all the attention it needs."

"So now you think I'm a whore. Do I look like a whore?" Oh bother, I had wanted to be polite, if I could!

"We are frequently visited by young women of good breeding who are supporters of some of my squad, and who wish to meet them face to face..."

"I know none of the men here, unless I have seen them on a rare visit to the *Flavian*."

"Be frank with me, then. What do you precisely mean by, 'I want to train here'?"

"You know what I mean."

There is a pause in the rapid thrust-parry, thrust-parry. He looks me in the eye, and I hold his gaze. Then he sighs, shakes his head, and offers me one of the chairs. We sit down, facing each other across the table.

"All right. You have come here because you imagine that you want to be a gladiator – no, let me go on – even though you know that women are fairly rare in this field. Maybe not unheard-of, but nonetheless rare. You have had some disagreement, no doubt, with your family, and rather than stamping around vowing to eat worms and die in a ditch, you want to make them sorry by throwing yourself into the arena, shaming them by association, making them powerless to save you, as they see you battling it out with a net-man at the next games. How right am I so far?"

"I... have no family."

"You're lying, but let it pass. Do you have any idea how many young people come to me and try this game on? Some are shivering in their shoes by the time they get this far, with the door shut behind them."

"You don't see me shivering, do you?"

"Others I kid for a while that I am taking them on. If it is a slack time for me, I put them through a day's training, with an instruction to my staff to be, well, moderately careless. After that, even if they are not begging to be released, I give them the opportunity of an open door. They take it."

"Why are you telling me this? Obviously because you know that I am serious. I am here because I want to be here. Because I want to stay here. Because I want to stay here as long as it takes me to win a wooden sword or..." I take a deep breath, and I can't help doing so, because of the enormity of the thought of not dying of old age,

"...or be carried out sandals-first!"

"Brave talk. The cheapest commodity in town! Yes, one or two people come here as volunteers. The odd one who is tired of being a free citizen and wants to bind himself to this particular unfortunate mystery. No woman has come to me in that way. The couple I have trained have been like most of the men – like my whole squad at the moment – slaves born and bred, or captured outlanders, or army deserters who preferred this chance of a longer life to being stoned to death. These types last the longest. Some free-born fighters make a half-way good showing, but turn out to be unlucky in the end."

"I take it this is a standard speech."

"No, I don't recall having made it before. I have a feeling that I am dealing with a special and unusual case. A very unusual case. A person of rare character. Someone that the free society of Rome could do with on the outside, rather than having her talent wasted in the microcosm of professional combat." He is doing me the honour of using long words, Greek words, to acknowledge that I am an educated person, and is doing it without irony. Also he is looking intently at my face, as if to memorise it, or search for some likeness to a well-known family. Aha! Thrust-parry, thrust-parry. I am beginning to enjoy this. *He* is beginning to enjoy it too.

Come on, girl. Relax. I sit back in the chair, and take a deep breath before going on.

"Honourable Lanista, you have tried to sound me out. You are now aware, surely, that I am neither a time-waster, a whore, a foolish girl with a crush on one of your men, or a youngest-daughter having a tantrum. You are aware that I am in deadly earnest – and I mean *deadly* earnest – about coming through the iron gates outside, dying to all I was, and living for as long as I may as a figure in a fish-mask in front of a clamouring crowd. You know I am bloody-minded enough to stick at the training, and not to be scared off by a day or so's shock. That is why you have bothered to see me, and have bothered to spend your time, while your dinner gets cold, giving me a debate which you have never given to anyone else who has come knocking on your door. You have done all this because I walked in here having taken on your two ham-fisted guards and cut one of them with a knife, despite my obvious breeding. You have done all this because you know that I am worth the trouble. You are not going to send me home, it's as simple as that."

Another pause. I notice how it has gone silent outside. The swallows have stopped screeching – the daylight is fading and they have probably started to roost, but it is as if they are listening in fascination to the thrust-parry, thrust-parry. The boss is looking at me. Once more I have to meet a steady stare with a steady stare. Eventually he breaks the silence, holding his hand out to the gatekeeper, who has been standing all this time at the top of the stairs, watching and listening to our conversation.

"Give me one of our special contracts."

The gatekeeper fetches a tablet from the shelf, and hands it to him. The Lanista almost throws it down upon the table between us, and pushes a stylus over to me.

"Enter your full name at the bottom of this," he says.

"I'll make a mark. I can't write."

"You're lying. You're an educated young woman. You lied about your family and you're lying now. Enter your name."

"And then I'll be here as long as it takes you to send old Cut-hand to the house of Senator So-and-so to tell him his wayward daughter is here! I'm not going to fall for that one either. So I'm lying, I lied about my family, and I lied about visiting the Flavian Amphitheatre too. I've been past Nero's sandals as often as I could. I know this place by its reputation. I know your squad is the best, which is why I came looking for this place. And I know what you're thinking now – that I must be from one of the families who have private seats, so I will be only a little harder to trace. Hard luck. I come alone and sit in the sunny seats. So, as far as our business is concerned, I can't write!" I take the stylus, and make a *chi* symbol at the bottom. Then I return it to him with as little ceremony as he gave it to me. By now, Bully-boy is open-mouthed.

"Just what has your family done to you?" asks the boss.

"You don't need to know. You don't want to know. Believe me."

He studies the mark I have made, and traces it with his finger. I must have made it deep, in my anger. Really, I am angry; my anger is as red as the sunset to the west, and as black as the sky to the east, which is threatening to spit rain at the city. Now I really am shivering, and I do not know whether it is this anger of mine, or the chilly breeze that is coming in at the window, now that the warmth of the day is over. He looks up from the tablet.

"What shall we call you, then?" he asks.

"*Infama,*" I reply, and he shakes his head at this suggestion.

"Everyone who comes into these barracks is disinherited and dishonoured, as far as the outside world is concerned. Some may live long, some may walk out of here, some may marry, some may amass riches, but each one lives a life devoid of real fortune, devoid of luck, devoid of the protection of any god except Nemesis; all end up in the hands of Anubis. You would be simply one *Infama* amongst many *infami*. For my money, you are *Lupa*."

For the first time since we came upstairs, Cut-hand speaks.

"She-wolf. I've felt her teeth. It's a good idea!"

"I didn't ask for an opinion," says the Lanista. He doesn't raise his voice, nor does he look at his man, but those few words are like a lash well laid on. Now I can see the nature of the man to whom I am binding myself. Now I can see what it is that gives him the kingship of this little kingdom. Without further ado, he stands up, at which I feel I must stand too. He addresses me:

"I have enjoyed this conversation. I know that you have too. You will never have another opportunity like this. You will never come up to this room again unless and until you are told to. You will never again address me with such familiarity. You will confine your excellent fighting spirit to the training ahead of you. You will never again lift one finger against any of my employees – from now on the slightest injury to any one of them will cost you your life. I will do you only one further favour, after which you will be like any other here – I will warn you that it is possible that things will be difficult for you as the only woman here. Now..." He turns to the gatekeeper, "...take her to her quarters."

He sits down and studies some documents on his table. For a moment or two, neither I nor bully-boy move. Without looking up, the Lanista says, "Go with him, slave!"

The last Rubicon is crossed with that one word, and we make our way down the stairs. I know now that he will ignore any hue and cry – if there will be any – about a missing young woman. I have done what I came to do. What have I done?

CHAPTER III

Next morning I had showered and breakfasted about forty-five minutes earlier than usual, and was sitting, in jeans and a sweater and with one ear on the radio news, when the phone rang. It was Vittorio. We arranged to meet at ten o'clock, at the very spot where we had parted company the day before. I put on my trainers, then kicked them off and went looking for an old pair of boots instead. I still felt that this was a game of sorts, and wanted to arrive a casual five minutes late. But I found myself hurrying, and as it happened a clock somewhere struck the hour as I was half way across the road. I scored a minor point.

Vittorio was waiting for me, dressed in what looked like mechanic's overalls and a tee-shirt, but both freshly laundered. He greeted me with a smile, which I returned. We hailed a taxi, and he gave the driver an address across the city. As we threaded through the morning traffic, he began to tell me about the dig. He was more animated than he had been the previous day; he seemed to be in his element as he described the site to me, and this made it easy for me to relax in his company. When the taxi stopped and we got out, I was surprised to see that we were in a landscape of building sites. It was difficult to tell whether this area had been, until recently, fields or condemned buildings – the latter surely, as we weren't far enough out for it to have been fields.

"There used to be a grove of pines here, on a small rise, or so we think. If you look over in that direction, you can see that the ground is not really level – it slopes upwards. They're planning to put up apartment blocks here. But someone spotted something as they were preparing the site, and I was called in. It appears that I have enough influence to hold up work for some considerable time!" He grinned at that thought.

"Anyhow, by the pine grove there seems to have been a graveyard, and we are beginning to think it was where gladiators were buried – because of the finds, and because of certain evidence from the bones of the people buried there, which show they have been, well, knocked about a bit. I got a call yesterday to say..." he paused and looked at me, "...that one of the bodies appears to be female."

"Female?" I raised my eyebrows.

"Yes. You're not the only woman in history to appear in an arena."

"Look, I'm not stupid." There I went again, that temper of mine. "I knew scores of girls and women in the circus. But if you mean she was a female gladiator, that's different. Couldn't she have been...well...a wife or a girlfriend? Or a servant? Does this have to be a burial site for gladiators at all?"

I have to admit that I was intrigued. Vittorio went on.

"It's not so strange, and I didn't expect you, of all people, to be caught by the trap of sexual stereotyping. All right perhaps that was unfair. I must admit that it wasn't an everyday thing, even in ancient Rome. But have you never heard of the famous Roman relief discovered at Halicarnassus, showing two females in gladiatorial gear? Their names were Achillea...and Amazonia! Yes, I thought that would make you take notice!"

Take notice? I had leapt round to face him, blocking his way, looking up into his face. He seemed to have twanged a sympathetic string inside me that I didn't know was there. I have never known my interest to have been aroused so quickly about something. An ancient fact had suddenly become more real to me than the two-dimensional city; like a fist bursting through a paper screen, the thought of the two women fighters grabbed me, winded me, and yet made me feel suddenly alive. I was not entirely comfortable with this reaction; it had come on like an instant drunkenness, almost as though I had suddenly realised that I had – I don't know – some sort of sexual fetish. Within the fascination was a little revulsion, and that spiked it up, made it intoxicating. Of course there was the coincidence of the names, so close. But that was an accident of modern Italian usage in any case. My professional name meant nothing more than Circus Girl or Bareback-Rider.

"But surely..." I didn't know what to say. There seemed to be no way to put into words all the thoughts which were now racing through my head, each one disappearing round a mental corner, gone as fast as another one came.

Vittorio waved to someone at the dig, who waved back; then he sat on a low, half-demolished wall, and made a gesture to me to sit as well. I found somewhere opposite him. I wanted to face him, not to be at his side. I wanted eye contact.

"The inscription on the relief reads: 'An honourable release from the arena'," he said.

I took a breath.

"You don't have any idea what it's like," I said to him. "You don't know what it is to have your everyday life suddenly turned upside down. Everything out there looks the same – your house is the same, the street is the same, the sparrows sitting on the fence are the same, the clouds in the sky are the same – but some very important things have changed. Like you're afraid for your life. You're afraid of your neighbours. You're afraid that your friends or your father will be killed. You're afraid *you* will be killed – or worse, you're afraid you'll have to endure life when you would rather *be* killed. I've been there. I've seen this. I've been trying to forget it, but I can't. All I've been able to do, until now, is avoid talking about it.

It's men. It's always men. They have the guns. Not the women. They come into your street in fatigue trousers and camouflage vests, and stupid bandanas round their heads. They come in trucks, and jump out, and start kicking all the doors in. Or they swagger round the corner with bandoliers over their shoulders, and kick in a selected few. Then they drag someone out. If it's a man or a boy, they kill him. If it's a woman, they rape her. Then maybe they kill her.

Maybe it's someone you know. Maybe it's someone you don't like. That doesn't make it less horrible to see. Maybe it's your mother or father that's being raped or killed. Maybe – and this is worst of all – the faces of the men with the guns are faces you recognise. Maybe a teacher, a baker, a plumber, a civil servant. Maybe the man in charge was the local librarian!

Who are they? It doesn't matter. They could be the people from the next town. Who cares if they are Croat, Muslim, Albanian, whatever. Who cares if they're even your own people, and they have found an excuse to hate you – you were friends with the wrong people, you didn't help round up so-and-so. It's men. Men. Men. I have seen them form a circle, and put someone they've captured in the centre. They give him a knife, and then one of them steps into the circle, and he has a knife too. I've seen a captive try to run away or break through the circle, only to be grabbed and pushed back in. I've seen a captive fight for his life, only to be butchered for his cheek. I've seen a captive dare to wound one of the men in fatigues, and then the others kick him to the ground, kick him to death, and then piss on his corpse. I've seen two neighbours forced to fight, with the promise that the one who wins and kills the other can go free, only to see the winner shot where he stood. Always men. Men. Laughing. Always laughing.

And the women? If there were women with them they were somewhere off to one side. Oh sure they egged the men on. Oh sure they called the captives all sorts of names. Croat bastard. Muslim faggot. Dirty Serb. Albanian shit. Do him, Goran! Stick him, Marian! But they didn't do the fighting, they didn't do the kicking down doors.

No. But sometimes when a captive was down, and desperate to be left alone or even to die, I've seen women take a knife and gouge out an eye or two, or take a testicle from a live man as a trophy. I've seen a woman cut another woman in a way that makes me sick to think about. I've been trying to forget all this, but I'm damned if I can.

But these men, they were the ones who stood up and fought. They were dirty, they were cruel, they didn't care who they fought, or killed, or tortured, or raped. But they were the ones that did it. They stood up and did it. The women sneaked around the edges and watched, or did some petty atrocity to one of the helpless. I've seen all this! I've been there! It's part of my life. Don't ask to see the other scars I have, apart from this one on my face, because some of them I just can't show you. Do you want me to go into detail about what happened to my own family – which of these nice scenes featured my mother and father? Or do you want to guess?

So – after all I have seen, how can you accuse me of buying some sort of sexual stereotyping? If there is a stereotype it is based on something which can be observed. And after all I have seen, how can I imagine two women going into a vast arena to slug it out with swords in front of a baying mob? And then getting some sort of honourable discharge at the end of it all? I can't take it in. It's just not real life. Life isn't like that."

It seemed as though I had said all that in a single breath. It had now run out. I was perspiring and trembling, but I fixed my eyes on Vittorio's, determined to stare him out and not to blink. I don't know why.

He was silent for a while, and then he said, "I'm sorry."

So I looked away. "There's nothing for you to be sorry about. I'm sorry I..." But I couldn't finish the sentence, and for a moment I was almost in tears, overwhelmed by what had come to the surface just then. The problem with trauma does not lie in remembering it, but forgetting it. One or two heads over at the dig had turned in our direction – obviously I had been louder than I realised.

"No, I am really sorry. I had no idea that all the troubles over there were so close to you. I had no way of knowing what you had seen or what you had gone through. Believe me, if anything I said brought all those memories to the fore again, I wish I could un-say it."

I pulled myself together. "Tell me about female gladiators. Tell me how you reckon it was possible to get women to fight in the arena. Tell me – yes tell me everything you can. It won't bring up any more memories. The memories are just there, and that's that."

"Well, what can I say? It appears they existed. And I guess your own attitude existed too – that women might sneak around the outside, but they didn't do the fighting. What else were all the women doing in the audience at gladiatorial fights? I dare say that the female hangers-on in the story you told me – almost told me – were hot for some of the guys in the Rambo outfits. I'm sorry again, I'm putting all this very badly."

"No, that's all right. Go on."

"They were scandalised and fascinated, all at the same time. Something like that. Imagine coming to a small arena in the provinces, the size of a modern Spanish bullring, or an open version of your own Big Top. You would have brought your own cushion along, as the tiers would have hard seats, and you would be crammed in with about seven thousand other people, overlooking a little ring which would seem almost small enough to stretch a hand out into. You could almost tell the colour of someone's eyes over at the other side. The names on everyone's lips would be Amazonia and Achillea, because those names would have been announced by criers all over town, and would have been up on notices everywhere. You would all have sat, bored, through the warm-up fights, which might have been little more than horse-play with wooden swords. What you were all waiting to see would be the unnatural sight of two women in hand-to-hand combat. How often in a lifetime would you expect to see something like that?"

I shuddered. Something had come into my mind which I had, after all, forgotten. I had been wrong about that. One evening, when a friend was driving me through Srebrenice, over to a house where I would be safe, we passed down a street in which several of the lights had been knocked out. We realised our mistake, too late – there was a group of men in fatigues, with guns casually slung over their shoulders, half-way down the street, under one of the remaining lamps. I remember that my friend swore, hesitated a little, but then continued driving, muttering, "Not too fast. Not too fast." Each time we passed a lamp, I could see sweat standing out on his forehead. As we drew nearer to the group, I saw that one or two of them had noticed us, and their unslung guns were now trained on our car. The rest were preoccupied. One of those knife fights was taking place – my friend had told me, "Don't look!", but I saw out of the corner of my eye that the cocky knife-fighter in fatigues, switching a long blade from hand to hand with leisurely ease while a man in ordinary clothes cowered awkwardly, was slightly built, and despite the boyish, black hair, was obviously female.

They let us pass. Or I wouldn't have been here in Rome, listening to Vittorio.

He was still talking. My attention had drifted away, and I must have missed some of what he had said.

"Now, you would all have been very grateful to the man who had paid for this entertainment. He might even have won your voices at the forthcoming election time."

An absurd phrase came into my head – something my grandmother used to say. "In my day we made our own entertainment." I was thinking about the home-made entertainment in the streets of Srebrenice.

"I beg your pardon?" said Vittorio.

I must have spoken the phrase out loud.

"Nothing," I said. "May I see the dig?"

CHAPTER IV

I am standing here in my room. I seem to have had one piece of luck so far, and that is this room. Most of the squad share; some sleep in a dormitory – the newer ones, who probably resent my luxury. As the lone woman here, I have been put in an unoccupied room. It has been fitted with two beds, but there is no one else here.

Here's another surprise – there is a bolt on the inside of the door! It's not a very substantial bolt, compared to the one on the outside, but in any case now I come to think about it, I did not hear Cut-hand slide the outer one across. Very quickly, I shoot it home, and sit down on the bed. Now I shake, now my teeth are chattering. What started as a controllable shiver as I walked back down the stairs from the Lanista's office is now an uncontrollable fit. I must lie down until it subsides, cover myself with a blanket, and see if exhaustion will overcome it. But really, the enormity of what I have done is only just hitting me.

Whatever happens, I must not beg the Lanista to let me leave – I don't think he would agree anyway. But if he left the door open, what would I do?

I said "another surprise". The first one was when I was crossing the yard, and I realised that no one had taken away my knife. Why not? I knew of no slave who went armed as a matter of course.

At another door, we entered the canteen. The whole squad, I guess, were in there eating. Many sat a long table, some sat in groups at smaller tables, one or two occupied a solitary stool, and spooned their rations from a bowl. I could have predicted what would happen next. Conversation stopped, briefly! Of course – a stranger had walked in, and a woman too. But there were already a few women in the room, some amongst the people who served the food, others sitting and talking to some of the squad members. What precisely were they doing here, I wondered. Everyone looked at me, some only briefly before returning to their food or conversation; there were one or two leers, and plenty of puzzlement. The most appraising looks came from the women, but I did not meet their eyes. I just scanned the room.

One man did maintain a stare, and his eyes followed me as I walked the full length of the room. He was one of the solitary ones, sitting on a stool which was backed into a corner. He held his spoon half-way up to his mouth. Stares today – always stares! No, I wasn't going to lower my eyes from this one, so I returned the stare until I stumbled and nearly bumped into Cut-hand. When I looked back, the solitary man was still watching me.

He was big. He had a bulk which seemed to be neither muscle nor flab. His skin was pale. His face was too bland to be ugly – it should have been the face of an idiot, but there was an intelligence in his eyes, maybe human, maybe that of a wild beast. I couldn't tell. His feet seemed to be too small for his build, and all of a sudden it came to me that he must be very quick on those feet, a dangerous man to tangle with, and solitary as much by the choice of the others as by his own. I thought there was something familiar about him, but I wasn't sure what it was.

Cut-hand led me right through the canteen. It occurred to neither of us that I may need something to eat. I certainly didn't feel hungry. My only thoughts were controlling the shaking, staring back at the big, pale, solitary man, and getting through the room to some place where I could simply slump and let go of the tension that was making me ball my fists. "Just let me have a moment or two," I thought. "Just a moment or two to be myself, get my bearings, settle myself, and then I will be able to cope!"

By the time we had passed through the dormitory,

down a corridor with several doors off it, and eventually to the door of this room, I had almost lost control. Cut-hand knew it, and was grinning. It was a relief when he shut the door behind me. My shoulders, which I had been holding rigid, sagged.

From my bed, I look up at the window. It looks out into the ring, but from this angle I can see only the moon. I try to remember a prayer to her, but the only god whose name comes to me is indeed Nemesis, and the moon turns into the face of the solitary man in the canteen. I am still shivering, but I feel warm under the blanket, and the bed is quite comfortable.

Have I been asleep, then? I can't remember shutting my eyes and drifting off, but now the room is filled with daylight, and there are noises throughout the barracks. I feel no disorientation, I know precisely where I am and why I am here. I sit up. I stand up and hold my arms straight in front of me - there is no shaking, no shivering. As I fasten my robe at the waist, so that it looks a little less like a fashionable gown, and shake my hair loose in order to tie it back in a simple tail low at the nape of my neck, I take a proper look around the room. It is no prison-cell, that's certain. It has been kept decorated and cleaned, there are a few boxes and a chest – empty, I find – and a shelf with a few items of both use and ornament on it. There are pegs on one wall, for hanging garments, or equipment perhaps. This is almost like a room in a hunting lodge, more than slaves' quarters. I had gone to sleep with my knife still in my waistband – lucky I didn't roll over and impale myself, so Nemesis is already looking after me – and now I nestle it into my left palm, with the blade flat against the inside of my wrist. This way it is possible to carry it near enough concealed, down beside my left hip. With my other hand, I pull back the bolt and open the door. Now I step out into the corridor.

There has been no stamp of feet, no rap at my door, no barked order to wake, but I feel it must be time to be up and about. What is it that makes this place run? There is a little coming and going here in the corridor, people making their way towards the canteen, and now I really do feel hungry, as someone opens the door and I can smell food. I am as ravenous as a she-wolf, that's certain, because I have not eaten since breakfast back at...

No, that was a million years ago, in a world that does not exist.

So I stride purposefully down the corridor and into the canteen. As I go across to the serving-table, there are no stares. I flip my knife round, stab a hunk of bread, and pick up a bowl and spoon. Where to eat? The long table seems to be the best idea, so I take a place at it. Someone asks me to pass down the water jug, and thanks me when I do. Someone else says it looks like being a fine day. Another fellow actually speaks directly to me, hopes I slept well, and apologises for the noise last night – there had been an argument over a dice game after supper.

"I slept like a baby. No problem," I say.

So this is what it is like in the barracks of one of the most efficient gladiator schools in Rome. Banal. I don't know what I had expected. One hears tales. The tales had originally fuelled my rebellion, rather than dampening it, and now I am beginning to feel a little disappointed. Will it always be like this?

*

We are all trooping across to the centre of the ring. I have my robe hitched into my waistband. Over to my left by an archway, I catch sight of the Lanista. He is nonchalantly studying a tablet – it might be mine. Through the archway I can see the door into the street. It is open, and for a moment I check my stride. Shall I change direction and head for it? As if reading my mind, the Lanista gives a brief gesture, and a gatekeeper slams the door shut. That's that, then.

I am here. No drama of a Gladiator's Oath. No shackles. I am simply here.

CHAPTER V

I set about researching. There were books in my friends' flat, and I knew where I could find a quiet internet café.

Gladiators were *"perditi homines aut barbari"* – outcasts, little better than savages – drawn mainly from the slave population or from captured soldiers and warriors of defeated nations. So how much lower could a woman sink, in a society whose outward mores praised virtue? I found that Suetonius wrote about torchlit games organised by the Emperor Domitian, in which women took part as well as men. Martial, one of Domitian's protégés, described events where women fought dwarves, to the great delight of the audience. Emperor Nero appears to have had a taste for spectacle also; according to Cassius Dio he organised a show at Puteoli for the king of the Parthians, where Ethiopians of all ages and both sexes fought each other. At other times he forced his political enemies, and their wives, into the arena to fight, despite their being of noble birth. Petronius, writing around Nero's time, described a show where a woman fought from a British chariot.

Emperor Septimius Severus prohibited the practice of

having women fight, so if he banned it, it follows that it must have been going on at his time! Maybe the number of women fighters had become a scandal in itself. Maybe the edges had become blurred between women fighters and men in some way; there was a class of fighters known as "the effeminates", men who fought in women's clothing, and perhaps this didn't fit in with Severus' idea of Roman virtue. He was, as it happens, from northern Africa, and could well have wanted to show himself as being more Roman, and thus more virtuous, than any native Roman.

What fascinated me more than the words of the classical writers were the archaeological finds, such as the inscription in Ostia, at the mouth of the Tiber, in which someone makes the boast that he was "the first since the foundation of Rome to make women fight". Or the piece of Samian pottery from Britain, inscribed with the name of "Verecunda", who was described by a word that could have meant dancer or fighter.

Vittorio had told me about a dig in London in 1996, and it was this one which fascinated me most of all, as it was the closest thing to the site his team was working on in Rome. I discovered more about it at the internet café. The London dig had turned up the skeleton of a young woman, about twenty years old, and intriguing grave-goods. There was a dish decorated with a fallen gladiator, and eight oil-lamps, three of which had representations on them of the Egyptian god Anubis, who conducted dead souls to the underworld. The grave-goods showed that she was not poor, and maybe this was a measure of her popularity in the arena.

I pestered Vittorio to be allowed to come to the dig every day. I could tell that he was slightly irritated by this, but too courteous to show it openly.

"It's not possible," he said. "The team need to get on with their work. We have a deadline which even I can't ignore. I can't hold up the building development indefinitely."

"I could help," I insisted. "I could be a volunteer at the dig. It would get me out of the flat – there are only so many times I can watch the same spaghetti westerns! I don't mind fetching and carrying if necessary."

"You're getting a little obsessive about this."

He was right, I knew. I could tell that a kind of manic excitement was building up inside me. But I wouldn't let go, and eventually he agreed to speak to the foreman of the archaeological team. He was a broadly-built man whom everyone called simply Signor Ciani; he in his turn called everyone by first names, except for Vittorio, whom he addressed as "Boss", in an almost mocking way. I fancied I could hear the quotation marks around the word, just like when a policeman calls me "Miss". Vittorio explained that it was really Signor Ciani's dig.

"I tend to specialise more in early Christian archaeology," he said.

I was not to be allowed on the site every day, but in fact I did make my own way there almost daily – I could get most of the way there by the Laurentina-Rebibbia underground line – when I was not at the internet café. I usually sat at the perimeter until someone called me over. I was not allowed to do any actual digging, or to work with a brush and trowel. As I had volunteered to fetch and carry, then that was what I would be set to do. I was to be their "gopher". I might, it seemed, be allowed to sieve earth from the dig, or to wash pottery finds.

So that is what I did.

Vittorio himself did not spend much time with me while he was there. He would greet me when he arrived, and before he left he would give me a run-down of what was going on. Sometimes he would offer me a taxi ride home, and would give me a thorough, if rather perfunctory lecture on the state of the dig. I always pressed him for more details.

"It's a painstaking business," he said to me, during

one journey. "Part of it is guesswork, because the picture is never complete."

Signor Ciani was usually fairly talkative, when he came over to where I was working, and some of the other team-members were friendly. They were mainly volunteers, or archaeology students. Others, professionals and people who were unimpressed by my credentials as a well-known circus act, were less so. I pestered everyone with questions. I couldn't keep my mouth shut. I gabbled and babbled so much that eventually one of the professionals looked up from his trowel-work and told me to get on with something useful or get off the site. I was brittle and bright at my sieve for the rest of the afternoon, and sung a little nonsense song, quietly – something we sang at the circus, all about Signor Polony the India-rubber Man – hardly realising, by the end of the day, that I had been singing it continuously for two hours.

The next day I didn't go to the dig. I got up, showered, had breakfast, got into my work clothes. Then I looked out of the window, and I didn't recognise the view. It was two-dimensional, flat, and unreal. The sounds coming up from the street seemed to be coming from miles away, or from under water. The sun was shining, but to me the sky was black. The buildings and the street were black, but different shades of black. People and cars moved, but in a series of one-second stop-frame. Everything was alien. Even inside the apartment too everything was unrecognisable, desolate, black upon black, unbearable. I sat down upon the floor, drew my knees up under my chin, and fixed my eyes on a black spot in the middle of a black wall. I felt as though I were hardly breathing.

Evening was falling, it seemed to me, and maybe the overall blackness was fading gradually into shades of grey, when there was a knock on my door. I must have made some sound in reply. When I am asleep I sometimes dream that I have opened my mouth to call out to someone. I try to form words, but my mouth is dry and won't work. Something approaching a croak might come out, but otherwise I am dumb. I knew I wasn't sleeping at that moment, but the words "Come in, it's not locked" simply died before I could speak them. I wondered whether the person at the door would go away, and whether I would stay where I was, ossified.

I must have made some sort of noise, however – a gasp or a whimper – because suddenly Vittorio was in the room. For a moment he looked at me.

"Come on," he said. He caught hold of my arm, firmly and gently, and hauled me to my feet. I realised how stiff I was, how cold. My head ached. I let him half-lead half-carry me to the sofa in the lounge, where he sat me down and covered my knees with a rug. I sat there, shivering slightly, while he moved quickly round the room, first switching on a table-lamp which made a soft yellow seepage in the greyness, then pressing a button on the CD player – the LED display drew my eye, more colour in the greyness, this time a few lines of green. There was a brief hiss as the VHF radio came on, off-station, while Vittorio rattled around amongst some CDs on the shelf. He found one, and put it on. Mozart's '*Soave si a il vento*'.

That piece doesn't last more than two and a half minutes, yet by the time it was finishing, Vittorio had been into the galley-kitchen, and had reappeared like a conjurer, with a mug of tea, made English-fashion, strong, hot, with a dash of milk. He turned down the volume on the CD player, and handed me the mug. The notes of the quartet faded away, and I burst into tears.

Vittorio sat down at the other end of the sofa. I really needed to be held, but he stayed at arm's length from me.

"Massimo sends his apologies," he said. "He didn't mean to be short-tempered with you yesterday." He meant the archaeologist who had snapped at me. I shook my head and sipped at the tea. I began to feel warm. The crying and the warmth of the tea made my nose run and I sniffed. Vittorio handed me a handkerchief. Another handkerchief.

"Thank you," I said, meaning for the handkerchief, on which I now blew my nose. "No, it wasn't that. I was being a pain anyway."

"Your choice of words..." he began.

"What?"

"Pain."

I thought I was done with tears, but now, as I began to say all the things which must have been building up inside me throughout the day, as I had sat motionless against the wall, I could feel that one tear would escape, stinging, from my eye and trickle down my cheek, to be followed by another one, and then another. I ranted in gasps, in incoherent lumps, in a chaotic, disjointed stream of consciousness. The words came from God-knows-where. The feelings behind them rushed out as if some growth in me had been lanced.

There were thoughts I never even knew I had. I told him that I would rather be freezing to death somewhere above the Arctic circle than stay any more in Rome. I spoke as if he had no idea – perhaps he did – of the rubbish that was spoken everywhere, of the pompous, moralistic dross in the newspapers and in the rest of the media. I put venom into the words "politicians and pundits", spluttering droplets of tea with each explosive p. "High-flown moral verbiage" – that was another phrase that fell off my tongue and collapsed into the air. I cursed all the media gurus, all the politicians, all the pop-philosophers "... every one of them making out he's from good, down-to-earth, Latin peasant stock, but that's just a façade for all the whoring they get up to with rent-boys!" Yes, I said that too. I was sick, I said, of their airs and graces, of the photos at home with family and golden retriever, and a bust of Marcus Aurelius on the mantelpiece. I had had enough of pavement-café philosophy – and the pitch of my voice went up here, as I clenched my teeth – in particular all the mouthing-off about what to do with all the Balkan asylum-seekers. "I'm over here for a holiday, I expect!" I shrilled.

I told him how every back street is filled with po-faced hypocrites, and that I had had enough. I was content to leave Rome to the sanitary engineers and building contractors – the type who swear black is white to get all the lucrative contracts, pocket the public money, and file for bankruptcy. Then – Hey presto! – before you know it they're back in business in their wives' names! Oh yes, I granted them that when it came time for the telethon they would be photographed with a cheque two metres long, for the sake of the publicity, but all they were really any good for was putting up the odd public lavatory – *si monumentum requiris, circumspice.* Maybe I was mixing Rome with London, but I didn't care! It was all some cosmic joke to me now, that people like that have always floated up from the gutter to become this year's beautiful people, shooting their cuffs, with trophy wives and all the trappings!

Words came after words, sometimes with no coherent sentence to frame them. I tore down the sugar icing of St Peter's, and filled the ruins with mobsters, bankers, and freemasons. I drummed my fists on the arm of the sofa until dust flew and my knuckles were red.

"What can I do here? I never learned how to tell lies. I never learned how to steal!"

"The great city," said Vittorio. It sounded like a Biblical quotation, and I thought it strange to hear that phrase from him.

"Sorry?"

"Nothing. It's too late to eat – the day's gone. You ought to get a good night's sleep. She who sleeps, eats," he said. "I'll go and walk around for ten minutes or so. Get into your night clothes and get into bed. I'll come and check everything is OK, and then I must get home myself."

I wanted him to stay, but that's how the day ended. A quarter of an hour later he smiled a good-night to me, left my bedroom door slightly ajar so I got a faint glow from the lamp in the lounge, reflected off a wall, and let himself out of the flat. His parting gesture had been to leave a box of tissues, a tumbler of water, and an apple by my bedside. A still life instead of a presence. I heard the front door click, and strained my ears to hear his footsteps, away into the distance. The noise from the nearby Viale Egeo was a low buzz, a barely audible rustling, like the sounds heard in the womb, and I fell asleep.

I think that was the first night I had the dreams.

CHAPTER VI

I have been here one year, or thereabouts. I do not keep a calendar in my room. I do have a couple of new robes, which I occasionally wear, but I prefer the male tunics that have been made for me, and are flattering enough whilst being practical.

The first six months of training are crushingly boring. If, at the end of this period, someone does not measure up, then he is sold. The Lanista will cut his losses, and sell to the first person who comes along, careless of how the failure will be treated, of whether he will be a household slave, a labourer, or what. Even six months at this place represent a considerable investment; we are fed well, clothed, and given medical treatment and massages, so a failure is regarded with contempt, and more or less thrown away. This place only trains people to fight in the great Flavian Amphitheatre!

I have begun to see how this place is run, by a single man with a handful of staff. It is by general acceptance of the culture. This is how things are. We do not break out, we do not rebel, we do not turn our knives on our masters. Life is hard, orders are to be obeyed, but it is our fate. The culture of slavery, of one person owning others, is deep in us, and not even the legends of Spartacus raise any resentment here. We don't go over the wall, because we don't go over the wall. There would be nothing there for us, it would be a world in which everyone around us was insane, or in which we alone would be insane. This is the world, right here, it is the only world we know – this and the games – and we have no mothers, no family, no citizenship, no existence anywhere but right here. The doors are locked at night, but a few good blows could perhaps loosen the hinges. Security seems more designed to keep people out than in, and the great gates serve as the bars of a cage in a side-show. Which is what we are, when we are not training or performing in the arena.

I have been surprised to find that there are one or two of our number who are well established and trusted enough to have a small house or a lodging outside the walls, where they live with a wife, in law or merely in fact, of several years' standing. Always they come back inside sharp at breakfast time, and do not leave until the day is well over. A couple of women live, with their husbands, in a room like mine.

One or two of our number are sometimes sent for, and are led away by an escort which may be a team of guards or a single household slave. This is rare though, as the

Lanista does not like it, and only allows it, for business reasons, in the case of a few clients of great influence. I overheard him once angrily remark to the emissary of a less prestigious enquirer that he was not running a brothel. Sometimes he sends one of us on an errand. We always come back. I say "we", but he has never sent me, and in fact he never sends one of us newer inmates.

We are a disparate squad. There are men from all over the empire. There are, however, no Germans and no Nubians – the boss does not like either race, and will not accept such newcomers, even in a job lot with a man he really wants. There are even a couple of men from outside the empire – one from over the Indus, in lands once conquered by Alexander the Great, and one a squat Asiatic – both of whom journeyed to Rome to do precisely what they are doing. Each of us is known by a single name – no patronymic or birth-name, just a catchy *cognomen*. As in any school of gladiators, there are men named for wild beasts – Lion, Bear, Eagle. There are names given in mockery of people of the past – here a Tarquin, there a Pompey, but no names of any Emperor, not even Caligula, because they have been deified. There are names which belonged to leaders of their races in the past – Vercingetorix, Caractacus, Hannibal. There are names from adjectives, describing their supposed fighting virtues – Ferocious, Swift, Strong. There are names given ironically – a diminutive Hercules, a broad-shouldered Mouse. There are names of mountains, rivers, and trees, sometimes a big bruiser rejoices in the name of a fragrant flower, and dares anyone to object to it. There are heroes of legend – here an Achilles, there a Hector. There are names based on hair colour – Black, Golden, Flaming. Sometimes a man of a particular race is given a pantomime name associated with his people – there are a number of Jacobs and Judes in this profession, for example, so many that they are often forced to break our rules and add an extra *cognomen*, and may be a Jacob the Mighty, Jude the Strong, and so on.

There is only one Lupa.

For the first six months, all our training is done in the ring. We are not put on show out in the yard – only fully-trained fighters go there to spar and drill, and that is as much a performance for lollygaggers and patrons at the gate as it is to hone their skills. No one would want to see us lubbers force our bodies into unnatural actions. For the first year we are worse street-fighters than we would have been if we had remained untrained. We are entrusted to one of the Lanista's lieutenants – now they *do* look like ex-fighters, muscled and scarred. They put us through our most basic paces; for weeks we did nothing but form lines, and routinely crouch in a single, fighting stance, rather like sitting in the saddle of a pony – down, hold it, up again, over and over – until we ached, in all weathers but the most inclement. Every day it was the same, until we were doing it mechanically, then one day the routine changed – down into a different stance, hold it, and up again. Then a week or so of switching between the two, and changing from having most of our weight on the right leg to the left and back again.

One day we formed our lines, and after a brief period of stance-changing, the instructor told us to make fists with our left hands, and imagine that our forearms were the radii of shields. Then he told us to make blades of our right hands, and imagine that they were the edge and point of a short sword, and took us through a few basic parries, cuts, and thrusts. Now for weeks we drilled at that, going through each movement, and each combination of movements in series of five, ten, and twenty. Sometimes he would tell one of us to sound off the numbers in the routine, and when he picked me, I would demonstrate my strength by bellowing them. It was a point of honour for me to show that I was tougher than the men, and would not be gasping for breath, and also a point of honour that when a few minutes' break was called, I would not flop down where I stood, or walk stiffly over to the ewer, but would sprint over and, cupping my hands, would take two swigs of water. Then, I would spend the break time keeping warmed up, and going through some of the drill as if to keep the proper technique in my mind.

Eventually we were paired up and taken through the routines facing each other, at which point we could see that some of these routines actually mirrored each other, a parry answering a thrust, a cut aimed at a momentary opening before being checked by another parry. For a while we went through these motions at a slight distance from each other, then in time we were ordered to step in close and make contact, and this is where it started getting difficult. There were cries of pain as arm clashed with arm, and if a man forgot the correct parry, he could get stiff fingertips in his belly, and collapse winded.

I suffered as much as anyone, and my sense of honour was in danger of collapse.

But still I sprinted for the ewer. This time the second handful of water was used to give a stimulation to my bruised forearms, as I rubbed them quickly before going back to my keeping-warm routine. One day, when I reached the ewer, I was surprised to find the Lanista himself standing there. What was more, he was without his toga, and was wearing a tunic not unlike ours.

"You've got bruises because you're doing it wrong," he said to me, then more loudly, looking around, "You all are! I had hoped that you would get the idea without being told, but I was wrong and you're all stupid. Now watch."

He motioned me out into the centre of the ring, and the others gathered around to watch.

"Routine number three," he said, and we went into it.

We hadn't gone through more than a couple of movements when I came unstuck in a big way. When I parried there seemed to be nothing to parry. When I cut or thrust, my right hand seemed to bounce off his left. I was flailing, and he was right inside my guard, cuffing me and jabbing me, forcing me to retreat rather than to stand and go through the routine. Yet he was doing the same movements as anyone else would be through this routine. And suddenly I saw! I got it! When he deflected with his shield arm, the motion was a seeking one, with a very slight angle to it. Cuts, thrusts, and parries were all made with a last moment of tension, and instantly a relaxation, so that his arms were less like iron bars than springy saplings, meeting blows with a yielding force which absorbed my energy rather than opposing it, giving blows in return that hurt but melted away. He could not be grabbed and pulled over while he fought like that, but his guard was always up, impenetrable. He never so much as perspired or panted.

"I can do that!" I thought, and tried to imitate what he was doing. He simply matched me, adapted to each reformed blow or parry, and stood his ground. But his eyes were bright, and he seemed to appreciate that I was getting the idea. When, at last, my right hand slid along his left arm, and neared his chest, he gave a great "Aha!", leaned forward, gave a slight extra push, and I sat down on the ground.

"Good," he said. "Master that." He said nothing more, but walked away.

His lieutenant told us that we better had master it too, because in a week or so we were to be allowed to work with weapons at last, and he expected very rapid improvement after that. So eventually we got hold of weaponry, albeit wicker shields and sticks for swords!

The banality of that first morning's breakfast was not typical, by the way. They were not used to me. There had been no female gladiator at that school during the career of any of the inmates. But pretty soon breakfasts became less placid affairs, and the conversation became coarse, as the men tried to see how much I could take. I remember one morning, a particular Illyrian boasted that his mother was a street whore, and he had cost his unknown father a couple of silver coins at most.

"That's nothing," said another. "I never knew who my mother was."

"Oh I knew *my* mother," said an Egyptian, with a mouth full of teeth. "She was raped at thirteen by a crocodile!"

"Will one of you bastards pass me the water?" I said, and they all laughed. It was a good moment. Later I put names to Illyrian, No-mother, and Croc, but those nick-names stuck too. I was Pass-water! Not that I particularly wanted to be one of the boys, and since then I have tended to spend meal-times at a smaller table, or on my own.

The big one still watches me. Now I know why he seemed so familiar. Although I had never seen his face, I had seen him in action in the arena many times. He was known as Moloch, named for the ghastly idol that eats children. He was popular, in as much as he was the man the crowd loved to hate. He would enter the arena in a grotesque steel mask, with tusks and black eye-holes, and as much of his unhealthily white skin exposed which was decent and prudent, given he faced armed opponents. He was indeed quick on his feet, also brutal and merciless, and he could bear down an enemy with alacrity, if he did not choose to play cat-and-mouse. He won all of his fights, and it was only because the crowd hated him that they let all his defeated opponents walk away. Now I think about it, I can't remember ever seeing him kill. A man does not need to kill – it seems – to be deadly.

I do not know why he watches me. No one else watches me, even in the bath-house. I tend to bathe during the quieter times, but nonetheless I can't reserve the place. It is just that I am no longer embarrassed to be naked in front of the men, nor they in front of me. No one whistles or makes a comment – the last one who did went to bed with one tooth missing – we just get in, have our bath, and get out. I have to admit I am not the young woman I was when I came in here a year ago. I have muscles on my arms, my face and limbs are tanned, and I have maintained a grim expression for so long that it must be set there.

Tomorrow is going to be a big day. We will be assessed for our weapons. Up to now, all our mass drilling has been with the idea, at least, of sword and shield. From now on we will specialise. Net and trident. Thrusting spear. Sword. Native weapons. From now on, we will live more and more in our own heads, closer and closer to our first public appearance. Nemesis, smile on me.

CHAPTER VII

Vittorio's therapy for me – he insisted on it, and I allowed myself to be led meekly along – was to ration my visits to the dig. Once a week from then on. I obeyed. He could be very firm, and had a kind of natural authority. Besides, he had seen me at my absolute lowest, and I felt as though this gave him some kind of right over me – I can't explain it, but that's how it felt.

On the very next visit, just as we arrived, Signor Ciani called him over. Most of the volunteers, along with one or two of the professionals were grouped around him, as he examined a small object in a clear plastic box. It was a find, of course, and I instantly felt jealous that I had not been there when it was uncovered, and that I had not been the one to clean the dirt off it. For a moment, I resented Vittorio's arbitrary authority.

As most of the others went back to their places, and resumed work, Signor Ciani began to describe the find to us. I could see that it was a little larger, by about twenty-five percent, than a Euro coin. It seemed greyish to me.

"Is it silver?" I asked, excitedly.

"Well spotted. Yes, it's silver. We found it – or rather Massimo did – just by the shoulder-blade of the female skeleton. It's not a coin. I think it's a medallion of some sort. One side is badly worn, and it's difficult to make out what's on it. It's most likely a symbol of a deity. But on the reverse there's an inscription. Here, Boss – your Latin is bound to be better than mine! Have a look."

Vittorio took out a small magnifying glass from an inner pocket of his overalls, and squinted at the object, turning it this way and that to get the best light. He frowned, and was silent for a minute.

"It says something like – 'Who can endure this monstrous city?'" he said. I wanted to echo the sentiment, remembering my outpouring of the other evening, but I bit my tongue.

"May I take a look at it?" I asked.

Signor Ciani smiled, and handed me a pair of latex gloves, which I put on. Vittorio held the open box out to me, and I carefully took out the little, round disk. I ignored the inscription and looked at the worn side. I could hardly make anything of it – there appeared to be a sweeping curve in the design, like a bow perhaps – so I turned it over again. How Vittorio could have made out the inscription, even with a magnifying glass, was beyond me. But I held on to the object, pretending to study it, but really I felt excited simply to hold something in my fingers that had come from *her* grave. I wanted to slip off the latex glove and actually feel it in the centre of my palm, as though I expected some kind of electricity to run from it. But Vittorio was getting impatient, so I handed it back to him.

"We'll have to send this away, to be looked at," he said. Then he turned to me. "Please excuse us for a moment. There's something I need to discuss with Signor Ciani."

Dismissed. I withdrew, and checked the holes in my sieve. They were all there, all in order. Vittorio and Signor Ciani were talking, *sotto voce*, with serious looks on their faces. Almost frowns. I wondered what was going on, what was so serious about this medallion, or whatever it was, that they needed this privacy to talk about it. One of the volunteers came by me, and said hello as she passed.

"What do you know about Vittorio?" I asked her, suddenly. She stopped and looked round.

"What do I know about *Vittorio*?" she echoed, with a little surprise. "Not a lot! Why? What has he told you?"

"Not a lot!"

She shrugged her shoulders, grinned, and went back to work. I had some earth to sieve.

Two days later, the second part of Vittorio's therapy started. He began to show me Rome – as he put it, "To add the missing third dimension." First he interrogated me about which places I had visited myself, as a sightseer, for want of better word. I told him. There were one or two notable exceptions to my list, which made him raise his eyebrows. I said I had considered them too banal – too "obvious".

"We shall see them nonetheless," he pronounced. "I can give you one day each week."

So that was decided. Yes Boss!

CHAPTER VIII

Now I have a calendar. It is important. I have to know what day it is. We are professionals, we who are taught to fight in the great Colosseum and reserved only for that amphitheatre. We are told as far in advance as possible when we will be fighting. I am fighting today. It is my first fight.

I have had an outfit custom-made for me by our armourer. I have a steel helmet, modelled on the Legionaries' Imperial Gallic. I have a body-shaped cuirass, and in my case they have exaggerated slightly a couple of features, and at least I could put these to some offensive use if it comes to close grappling. There is no back to the cuirass, only some leather straps, and my *pteruges* are short, so as to show off my legs. They don't miss a trick! I have greaves to match the breastplate, and hobnailed sandals.

Long ago, or so it seems, I was assessed for a small targe, in imitation of a standard-bearer's shield, and a short sword. That's how I like it, that's what I had hoped for. I never forgot the Lanista's lesson, and put it to good use with the practice weapons, to the point where I don't think anyone else from the comparative newcomers can touch me, and some of the veterans would think twice. I have been enjoying myself, honing the skill I first learned from the boss himself – he has never come back to the practice ring since that day – and when I had mastered it, I set about adding the flamboyant and exaggerated movements that add nothing to the fight but everything to the show.

Today is something different. Up to now, if I had suffered any sprain or cut, the instructor would call time and there would have been a masseur or a surgeon on hand to help me out. Today I am going to put my life on the line, and face someone who is really trying to stick a steel weapon in my body. Perhaps no one will call time. I might get killed – can I face that? I might have to kill – can I face *that*? A damned stupid question! But no matter how hard I try to focus, I have still had to go and sit on a bucket so many times that I hardly imagine I have any insides left!

Early this morning we formed up in the yard, in ranks of five, in full armour, even those of us who were not due to fight. The gates were swung back, and we were marched the two thousand paces or so to the amphitheatre. This was the first time I had ever been outside, since the day I first slashed Cut-hand's wrist for him. There he was, opening the gates. Off we swaggered at an easy pace, so that the public lining the route could see us. The roads were lined. People pointed out their favourites, the famous horses of our stable as it were, and speculated about the new figures in unfamiliar armour. Mine brought a few shouts, but I held my head up and maintained that expression of grim disdain.

The only one of us not in the ranks was Moloch, who walked alone, with a little armour-bearer staggering behind with all his equipment. The crowd lining the route was only held back by their fear of him. Occasionally he would turn to the right or left and spot a gaggle of younger people in the crowd. Then he would make as if to advance towards them, with a menacing crouch, arms spread out to clutch them, and perhaps he would let out a roar from inside his helmet. The youngsters would scream, and their fathers and older brothers would howl in anger, and hold each other back from mobbing him. It was all show, but they more than half believed that he ate children.

Our procession held their attention as far as the gamesman's gates to the amphitheatre, which slammed behind us as we entered. Security is much tighter here than at the barracks. Not all gladiatorial contingents have such a king as ours, such an adherence to our culture. There have been breakings out, and we hold ourselves aloof from this, as it is against our code of conduct. Nonetheless, we are held amongst the hustle and bustle, the machinery and properties, the animals and men of rival schools ("Ha! Who can tell the difference!" we jibe, in their hearing. Don't we care that one of them may be matched against one of us today?). Then waiting, waiting, and more waiting – that's when I visit the bucket – can't they get things started? How strange that until today I, and many of us, had been simply alive and concerned to stay that way, just like anyone on the outside. Now, when it was possible that some of us would not be coming back to the barracks, we just wanted to get our bout over and done with, and if we came back in a sack, so be it.

A visit to the shrine of Nemesis would be good, before I go on. Don't let me forget! I am waiting here in the half dark to be called. Outside, I can hear the noise of the crowd, only a little muffled. Focus, girl, mind on the task.

There was a tree by our villa, when I was a little girl. It was gnarled, and had branches that stuck out at angles. I used to think that it would be easy to climb, but for a long while – at any rate it seemed long to me – I was too little, and could barely haul myself up to cling onto the lowest branch. But one day I wasn't so little, and got up to the next branch, and to the next, and so on higher and higher. I remember the smell of the sap in the twigs I broke getting a hand or foothold. I remember the blackbird that suddenly flew from the tree in a panic, startling me and nearly making me let go. I remember the breeze, which made the leaves shimmer in the sunlight, and the shades of green that they cast. Above all, I remember that I could see for miles. It seemed to me that I could see over the whole world from this tree, even though it probably was no higher than one and a half storeys of the villa. I was entranced, and stayed until my body ached from hanging on; I was the tallest girl in the world. I ate some of the berries from the tree, just to see what they were like. Then I tried to make my way down, but it was not as easy as coming up, and I scratched my face and arms and began to cry. My cries became hysterical, and my mother and father came to rescue me with a ladder. When they had got me down, they did not punish me. The shock, and the slight stomach ache from the berries were punishment enough. My father carried me into the villa, into a cool room, and laid me on a bed. My father – I haven't thought about him for years now, and really I can't remember his face. I was so young.

My name is called! For a moment I do not move,

because I my thoughts were in a time and a place long before I became Lupa. Then I jerk into action and set off up the tunnel towards the gate. Oh hell – I've gone right past the shrine! Can't be helped. Up to the gate, out into the arena.

I remember to narrow my eyes for a minute, to give them time to get used to the sunlight, and it is bright. But at least I am remembering my lessons! Now girl, walk into the centre, never mind looking around you. But I can't resist sneaking a glance to fix where the sunny seats are, where I used to sit, and of course the glance becomes a full-circle sweep, because the place looks so different from down here. I shall stop where I am for now.

I am being joined, from another gate, by my opponent. He is a young tribesman from somewhere south of the limit of our empire in Africa. His face is impassive, but I can't help grinning at him because, after all, he is a comrade of sorts. Oh how my mind is running into silly things. Stupid, stupid girl! He is taller than I am, and is wearing a simple mail shirt. His weapon seems to be some kind of stabbing spear, about as long as he is tall. It has a long blade with a point, and one edge is sharpened – I haven't seen anything like this before, how can I counter it? I look down and notice that there is also a metal butt, so I guess that he must be used to reversing it as well as using the blade, and my mind is now racing to think of some possible moves to avoid either end of the weapon.

We both turn to face the tribunal, and walk forward to salute the President of the Games. It isn't even the Emperor, just some senator or other. I get it now, anyway, they are pitting a young African, with the supposed physical attributes of his race, against a virgin. A virgin in the arena, I mean. We both raise a hand in salute – just to show I get the symbolism, I raise my shield arm as he raises his spear. I wonder if he has fought before, or is this going to be a battle of two virgins?

We move apart, and stand facing each other. The arbiter, with his staff raised, stands between us. Out of the corner of my eye I see the president give a signal, and the arbiter steps swiftly away. Let it begin.

My opponent starts to circle me, and the noise of the crowd increases. He is like a man hunting game, and just for now I am like an immovable rock. Except that as he circles, I shift my stance so that I am always facing him. I cover myself with my shield, and hold my sword high, and a little wide. For a moment I think back to the day I approached the door to the barracks, and the stance I adopted when facing the two thugs with my knife. It was this one – I had seen it used at the arena, I had never learned it at the school. All I can think about is hiding behind this shield, and keeping this sword ready for a thrust or a slash.

This will never do. I have been in crowds that have grown restless at the sight of two fighters who do not get to grips with each other. We are not doing ourselves any favours here. If we don't sort ourselves out, one of us could end up dead and the other sold, and I do not know which would be worse. At this moment there is a real sense in which we are indeed comrades. We have to put on a show. Already I can hear shouts of "Get on with it!"

Let's force the issue. My next shift of stance actually brings me nearer to the African, and the knowledgeable sections of the crowd can see what I am doing now, and shush anyone who is still cat-calling. Another shift, closer still, and now he realises too that I am trying to close on him with stealth. He's game for it, because he stops circling, and takes a pace straight for me, holding his weapon easily in both hands, keeping the point towards me. Now I dance a little on my toes, and give a little stamp, almost a feint. This gets him moving, as he is within thrusting range. Thrust-withdraw, thrust-withdraw, I try to parry but I meet thin air. Then he shifts his grip, gives himself more reach, reverses the blade quickly and hacks at me from my left-hand side.

I spring back and he follows up, jab-jab. My parries meet air again! Jab-jab, and this time I turn one of the thrusts away with my shield. Jab-jab again, and I am backing away even though I have the measure of these thrusts now. I am not using my sword at all, it is still held back as I lead with the shield, and now there are some dissatisfied cries from the knowledgeable, which are taken up by the ignoramuses. Right then – I can tell by the way he has tensed himself that the next jab will be more of a deliberate lunge, so he is obviously no veteran if he announces his moves like that! So instead of parrying with my shield, I step forward, and use a risky, circling parry to push his blade away to my left.

Now we have closed, and I am using sword-shield, sword-shield against blade-butt, blade-butt, up and down; and this is more to the crowd's taste, because the noise is building. Nevertheless, we are both still thinking in straight lines, and he is pushing me backwards. I have to risk something here, or I will be pushed backwards and backwards until I can go no further. I do not want to have to worry about how close I am getting to the wall! So – just let me get inside this next thrust.

I have done it! But his mail shirt turns aside my sword

blade and, I notice now, his weapon has glanced off my cuirass at the same time. If we had both been naked, we would have both been dead now! As it is, we seem to be evenly matched, we virgins.

He has seen this too, and it has made him pause. I do not pause as long as he does, though, and begin to rain blows upon him. Shield-edge, shield-boss, blade, tip, pommel, bang-bang-bang and he is the one being forced back now, parrying me higher and higher and hardly striking a counter-blow.

Now I have him by the wall, and the people of this side are standing up and craning their necks to see. His parries and (now) counter-thrusts are wild, but not inaccurate – I think I have the better of him, but...

It is no good settling things on the edge of the arena. To the folk on the far side we are just toy figures. Hardly anyone on our side can see us here. I push him back against the wall and dance away into the centre. I know I am letting him gather his wits, but it is show time!

I stand there. Instead of taking up a fighting stance, I am standing erect, hands on hips. He is looking at me in amazement. I know what to do. I raise both arms high in the air, and I, Lupa, howl!

The crowd is going wild! They take up the howl, they are all standing in their seats, never having expected anything like this from a novice. My opponent enters into it and makes a charge. I barely have time to recover my fighting stance when we clash. The force of his charge carries me over, my sword goes flying away in one direction, my shield in another. Even my helmet is off. He recovers, and drives his weapon hard for me. The only thing near me is my helmet, and I clutch it desperately in my left hand and batter his thrust away. It was such a determined thrust that he can't pull back for another go, so I back-hand him across the head with my helmet, and knock him flying.

I resist the urge to jump astride him and keep battering him with my helmet. Besides, he still has that wicked spear. Quickly, my sword is there – a few strides and I have it. My shield – a few strides more. Now I am armed again, but helmetless, and I close while he is still clearing his head. We slam blows at each other. He is aiming to catch my unprotected head with the iron butt of his weapon, and he is not paying attention elsewhere – I duck and wallop him behind his knees with the edge of my shield. He goes down on one knee, but still has that deadly spear – now he slashes at my legs with it, and I am forced to jump over it. Now he slashes back, and I have somehow timed it so that I land on the shaft. It breaks in two. The crowd is yelling. He has turned his shattered weapon into a short sword and a club, but now I sweep them away with one scything swing of shield and sword together, and kick his leg from under him.

Flat on his back, he tries one last back-hand swing with the bottom half of his spear, but I catch his hand, and put my foot against his neck. He can't move, but my sword-hand is free, and my sword is pointing at his throat.

He raises his left hand in a gesture or surrender, an appeal for mercy. It is not for me to accept surrender, nor to give mercy. I look up at the President of the Games. He looks around at the crowd. All but a few realise that my opponent has fought well, and almost had me. He gives the sign for life, and I let my opponent up.

It is all I can do to resist giving him a pat on the back, and thanking him for the sparring session. But we have nothing to do with each other, and he walks off with as much dignity as a man can who has just been defeated by an equal.

Me? I raise my arms to the crowd and I let *them* give the wolf howl, as I walk back to the open gate.

*

Not many people realise just how many gladiators

simply walk away from fights. It is more usual than not, because after all we are expensive. I have been told that this is not something one thinks about before going in to fight. The professionals who have made it up from the provincial meat-yards, where life is cheap, are a different matter. They spit at the very idea of being allowed to live, of fighting to live. I am told they neither give nor ask for mercy, but rather a quick death with the name of their favourite god on their lips. It is the last thing on my mind just now, all this. I am a first-timer, I have barely beaten another first timer, I could not have taken on a veteran from the killing yards at the edges of the Empire.

At the bottom of the tunnel I find the Lanista.

"Clumsy, undisciplined, unimaginative, and lucky. You'll be dead within a year. Double training tomorrow," is all he says.

"Yes, boss," I reply to his back. But I am grinning. I am alive. My knees are beginning to buckle; tomorrow my bruises and sprains will hurt. But today my name is known!

CHAPTER IX

So my week became governed by a schedule, based around two days of activity – at the dig and around the city. In between those days, periods of let-down and renewed anticipation, taken up by sitting at a screen drinking endless lattes, down at the internet café; or surfing satellite TV for another western, if I was desperate.

Vittorio turned up for what I was trying not to call our next 'date', wearing his well-cut suit. It occurred to me that I had never seen him in anything other than this suit, worn with a sober tie, and the overalls he wore to the dig. He never appeared in, say, chinos, a casual shirt, a sweater carelessly draped round his shoulders, his Ray-bans perched on his head. He would have suited American loafers, a roll-collared shirt in lemon, a Fred Perry. I created a whole wardrobe for him in my mind, in shades of amber and softly-aged denim; I imagined him in a lightweight summer jacket, and a Frank Sinatra trilby. But there he was, at the street-door to my apartment block, as if that time he had come up to the flat had been an exception, a mistake, something which was not going to be repeated – and he was wearing the suit. I wanted to ask him if it was the only one he owned.

I had done the tourist thing on my own in Rome. I had sat in cafes, and I have been shopping, and I had been bored silly. Most the places Vittorio took me I had seen before, but some I hadn't. In his company, the familiar began to take on a new character, and the new was a delightful surprise.

It is not simply that he was an attractive man, and that I felt like someone special when we walked along together. There was something else. He walked through the city with some kind of authority, like an old-time consul or senator. No, it wasn't that. It was more dangerous. It was as though crowds would part slightly for him; conversation didn't precisely stop, but was more subdued in his presence. He seemed to generate a kind of unasked but understood deference wherever we went. I told myself that this was nonsense, and often when I tried to test this feeling it melted under my scrutiny, and I almost became convinced that it had been my imagination. But the impression that I had been walking the streets of Rome with a leopard on a chain – and that it was the leopard who was doing the leading – would not leave me alone.

"You're not falling in love with him. You haven't fallen in love with him!" I told myself. Maybe I hadn't, but I still felt the need to repeat this as a mantra. Nothing in his bearing or behaviour, except perhaps for the fact that his eyes twinkled and one eyebrow sometimes arched sardonically, ever suggested that he was flirting with me at all. Yet he sought my company twice a week, and seemed to take pleasure in showing me the city I thought I already knew, and thought I hated. His behaviour was almost mockingly correct; he never touched me, except sometimes to take my elbow, in an old-fashioned way, to help me step over some obstacle. He would open doors for me in an unaffected way, and the fact that he checked both ways to see if anyone else was coming and, if there was someone, would allow them through too, diffused and defused any hint that he was patronising me. I tried to hold his arm sometimes as we walked along, but he, with ease and with the deftness of a professional magician, could gently manoeuvre it so that I wasn't any more, and he could do it without making me feel rebuffed. I often wondered whether he was married, or gay. He fascinated me, but I always held back from asking him questions, as if my curiosity would cause him to disappear.

When he gave me an impromptu history lesson, I could hear and feel the forum bustling, I could see Marcus Aurelius on his horse; Rienzi, Buonarotti, the

Borgias, and Benito Mussolini suddenly appeared in my mind like living people. I can't even begin to explain how he made it happen. It was as though he had always been here, as though he had been part of Rome since it was a set of bare hills, as though he had eaten and drunk the city since infancy. Now he was part of it, or it was part of him. "Romantic bunk," I said to myself, but I wasn't wholly convinced.

Late in the afternoon of our first day's sightseeing, we approached the Colosseum. This was not my first visit – I had 'done' the place several times before – but I had not expected it still to be open; and indeed most people were coming out as we arrived. Again there was this impression of deference expected and given as˙ we walked though the entry gate, I following him not quite like a Japanese wife, not quite like an Italian daughter, not quite as if I was with him. We walked right into the interior of the place, down below what was once floor level, and still he walked ahead. We came to what I felt was its very heart, as if we had found the centre of a maze. That was when he stepped aside into the half-shadow, and with a simple gesture motioned me to stand a couple of metres away, opposite him. A shaft of reflected light fell across my legs, and my ankles felt warmer than the rest of my body. Vittorio said nothing, but stood there. He looked around easily, looked up at the sky, looked again at the walls. For a moment only his gaze fell on me, and I felt a breeze nibble at my shoulders at the same time, as if conjured by his look. Then he turned his head away, looked more downwards, and gently crooked his left hand round his right wrist. He stood almost as if in prayer, and that seemed as it should be, because one of the deepest shadows on the ground was cruciform. I looked up to check what was throwing it, and found that two metal bars rested against each other, across the small space that was open to the sky. They did not form right angles against each other, and though this made it plain that they had fallen together not by design but by accident, they seemed – this is the only word I can use – perfect.

Vittorio stood silently. What I could see of his expression was somehow sorrowful, even penitent. It was the face of a man who had broken some sort of rule or code by being here. At least, that's what the expression said to me. But I too felt as if I was breaking some sort of rule by looking at him, and I stopped doing it. Instead, I looked down at the shadow on the ground, and as I stared at it, I became aware of how quiet everything was. So I strained my ears to hear some sound of the city outside, but found that I couldn't. The breeze that had chilled me a few moments before had gone, and the air hung. Did we stand in a still pool of something that was outside time? The silence was utter, and at that moment ten thousand ghosts walked by, making my neck prickle.

Then the breeze came again, the moment had passed. Faintly, I could hear the city again. Vittorio and I looked at each other. His face was no longer penitent; in fact there was a calm, almost blank expression there, too gentle, too subtle to be satisfaction, but to me it meant that we had truly shared something. Without a word being said, we turned and retraced our steps all the way to the entrance, and into the reality of the city.

There was another time when I was with him – I remember now. Now, as I write this, it seems to have happened on the same day. But it can't have been, because this memory belongs to a hot afternoon. What confuses it in my mind is that we walked single file again, and there was shadow and silence. We were in an alleyway. It was tall and narrow, and made me imagine that I was in the Siq at Petra. The dusty ground muffled our footsteps. Back home an alley like this would be squalid, but here the dry air made the flaking, powdery plaster on the walls smell like a forgotten room in a museum, and look organic. I remember squinting upwards. There were a few windows, and some were open; from this angle, there was only the suggestion of a room inside, but such a room might well be in another dimension, for all that I could actually see. I reached out to touch the wall at each side, and my fingers slid over the rough surface as though I was caressing a floured baking-board. We moved slowly, in a dream-state, and the yellow, vertical stripe ahead, which was the exit from the alley, seemed to come no nearer.

Then suddenly we emerged, and everything was excitement and noise, and a fine spray of water replaced the sere atmosphere we had been in moments before. There, amidst the babble of tourists, amidst all the colour and noise, sparkled the Trevi Fountain. I stood there. It's too silly to say 'transfixed' – but I was pinned like a specimen butterfly. Why had I never been here before? How had I missed this magic experience? Why, as I blinked to get used to the sudden sunlight, was I grinning? As these questions bubbled in my mind like the water in the fountain, I found one for Vittorio.

"How did you know I had never been here?"

"You never spoke of it," he said. Then he challenged me with a question of his own: "How could you possibly have been here, if you never spoke of it?"

We stood, on the edge of the crowd, and I took in the

whole scene. People were throwing coins into the water. Vittorio made no move to do so himself, but gave a little gesture as if to say that I was welcome to. I shook my head.

"I don't do this sort of thing. It's too superstitious."

"It is. No more do I."

Again it was a moment of sharing, and we continued to stand and watch until our eyes had drunk their fill. Then we moved on. His behaviour continued in its correctness, but I think there was an ease after this, born of intimacy, of something approaching friendship, of something we both understood without saying so.

Later he asked me, "Now how do you like Rome?" I didn't say anything in reply. I did, however, begin to confide in him about my dreams. They were unbelievably vivid, and although in them I inhabited a world that was alien to me, that world somehow made sense. It was solid and consistent, and I seemed to belong there. In normal dreams images flow in and out of shadows and nonsense; by contrast, these dreams of mine were more like another life.

Whatever Vittorio thought about all this, he said nothing. He simply listened, like someone who had had years of practice listening.

CHAPTER X

There are days and times of days when we are allowed to lounge in the yard, and to attract the attention of passers-by. This is one of them.

Some of us go through sparring routines, as if to let the public have a little taste of our trade secrets. Some of us bring out a stool and sit in the shade. Some stroll up and down. By the end of the day, the haphazard footprints I first saw on the day I arrived here tell that day's confused story. We are not allowed to sleep on the ground, or to indulge in any lewd displays, or to shout loudly, or to get drunk. Conversations with the public and with each other must be held in muted voices.

"Miss, may I speak with you, please?"

I have been pacing up and down, as I usually do. Frowning. Thinking. The politeness, the formality, and the fact that he addresses me as a young woman of good upbringing brings me out of my mood with a snap. He has to be talking to me, because there are no other misses on my side of the bars.

Even so, I look around a few times just to make sure that I am the only woman here. Now I walk over to him. I say nothing. I simply look into his eyes. He has, I am sure, nothing I could possibly want.

"I believe you are Lupa. Am I right? I have been hoping I might get an opportunity to meet you."

"That is an ambition easily satisfied, then."

"My further ambition is to speak to you for a while, and perhaps to get to know you better."

"You don't want to know me, let me assure you."

"I assure you I do. You're very blunt. I have been a blunt man in my lifetime, a soldier – a junior officer, in fact, who did not make it very far up the chain of command, through being blunt of course. Bluntness is a virtue of sorts, but one that seldom reaps rewards. What is your name?"

"You know what it is. Lupa."

"I mean your real name, the one given to you by your parents."

"I was a foundling."

"Why did you drop your eyes when you said that?" he said.

More to the point, why am I putting up with this? I look up again, and see that he is smiling, and that it is actually a pleasant smile. He is not young, nor old; he is dressed in a smart toga, in which he holds himself with some pride. There is nothing remarkable about his face – handsome enough in a forgettable way – but there is something familiar about him. I suppose he reminds me of the boss, in a distant and better-humoured cousin sort of way. I look him straight in the eye again.

"Is this about sex?"

To give him credit, he doesn't laugh! I have been pestered for sex before, and have made it plain to all pests I'm not interested. I don't dislike the idea, it's just there are ideas that I like more. There's sex, and then there's sex.

"When I look at you," he says, "I see a woman in her mid twenties. Tanned and muscled, with long, dark hair. She is wearing a man's tunic, but has a grey cloak tossed casually over her shoulder in a way no man would wear it. She is handsome, but doesn't smile much. She is much more handsome than many women who do smile. Nevertheless, no, this isn't about sex."

Damn, I'm smiling now!

He gestures in the direction of a servant, who has been hovering at a respectful distance. The servant is carrying two camp-stools and a games board. Fox and Geese. "Do you play?"

That tree, by our villa, spreading its green branches over a blanket that had been laid on the ground. My mother, letting me win at Fox and Geese. A very old memory – like something that happened to someone else.

"Yes, I play. I mean, I did once. Long ago."

"Let's see if you remember." He makes a more definite gesture to the servant, who brings over the boards and stools. Can I find a seat for myself? – there's one over by where Moloch is sitting, in the shade. I fetch it, and Moloch watches me every step of the way. My life seems to be lived under someone's gaze all the time, and my only choice is to meet the gaze or ignore it. This time I ignore it. Let Moloch watch all he likes, there will be nothing to see. I simply pick up the chair and carry it back to the gate, setting it down opposite the stool with the board set out on it.

As we play – no, he doesn't let me win, but I am remembering enough to have him on the run a few times – we gather a small crowd, both inside and out. We are a diversion for other people, and I snap at the knot of gladiators around me, "You're in my light!" They step away.

As they walk off one shrugs, and another says, "I see Pass-water's passing ice today." It is not fear of me that makes them walk away, it's just that we all pick our time and place for company, to balance the fact that there are important occasions when we have no control over time, place, and company. The dispersal of the men on my side of the gate seems to have an effect on folk on the other side too – they melt away, leaving my visitor and me to our board and pieces. I win a game, and lose several. The afternoon passes. Once I drop a piece, and as I bend to pick it up, I can see that Moloch is still watching. Has he been staring all this time?

"We should rename this game Wolf and Geese," my opponent says. "Geese once warned the Senate that Rome was being attacked by invaders – that's me, an old member of Rome's goose-flock. The she-wolf, that's you. The founders of the city were suckled by a she-wolf."

"Oh I see, this is about sex after all! I shall have a word with our armourer, and he will make me a less demonstrative cuirass." Now we both laugh, and there's a strange thing – you see, I don't think I have laughed properly since I was an infant, and even then my memory may be playing tricks on me. We stand up.

"I have enjoyed this. May I come again?" he says. "My name is Patricius, by the way."

"Come if you wish, yes. I've enjoyed it too."

He turns to go, and I say, "Eunice."

He gives the stools and the board to his servant, and motions him away, then he comes back to the gate and stands opposite me. I look over my shoulder, and see that we are alone now, except for Moloch who is still sitting, watching.

"Eunice. That's a Greek name. You don't appear to be Greek."

"It's my grandmother's name. She was Greek. My mother was half Greek, and I guess that makes me a quarter Greek. Anyhow, my mother always used to call me by her name – I was Little Eunice to her – I never knew grandma. I have a proper, full name, but that's for high days and dressing up, and I don't dress up any more. Not quite true, because when I do dress up I'm Lupa now. Call me Eunice, if we're going to be that familiar." This is more than I have said in the whole of the afternoon. Why am I telling him all this? Why do I go on?

"My mother and father died when I was very little. I hardly remember them. Again that's not quite true, because there are some things which are very sharp in my mind, like the tree outside our villa. Not their faces, though. They died – plague, fever, illness, I don't know – very suddenly anyway. And somehow I ended up as part of my uncle's household. That's the best word for it – part of his household – because I have been as little regarded as a slave, so much so that these bars here make me feel more free than I ever did there. He resented me. One thing I do remember about my mother and father is how much they loved me. Not my uncle. To him I was just an encumbrance, and extra mouth to feed. To his three boys, my cousins, I was a little kid they had no time for. After a while it became their sport to torment me, day after day. Then I became old enough to do work around the house – they had few slaves, and my uncle said I should work for my keep. He beat me too."

"Your aunt?"

"Uncle was a widower. Considering he had his own house and had inherited my father's villa, he seemed to be in penury all the time. Maybe he was just close with his money – I never saw him go thin! Then I began to turn into a young woman, and the ideas turned from tormenting and housework to something else. That's why I started carrying a knife. I slept with it too. Sometimes that worked, sometimes it didn't. I used to dream about slitting all their throats, or of setting the house on fire. Then one day I came to the games, and it was as if my eyes were opened. I slipped away from the house time and time again, just to come and sit in the sunny seats and watch the men fight. It was exhilarating, even the deaths were exhilarating, even though some of them were pitiful. On the way home I would find myself imitating the fighters' movements – I got some odd looks from people! But something about the gladiators gave me teeth, and next time any of the family bothered me or tried to beat me, I bloodied them. The beatings and the abuse stopped, but my uncle told me that as far as he was concerned I could go to hell. I came here instead. I volunteered. I don't know whether they have ever seen me in the arena, and I don't care. I hoped one of their neighbours has recognised me and made them leave town in shame. I hoped they all fell off a bridge and drowned! Now I don't care about them at all. If you ever meet a fat widower and his three sons, and they ask about me, tell them I don't care. I don't care about them, or about anybody, or about anything!"

I have run out of breath. Patricius stands for a moment or two, and then says, "I shall come again. Next week, perhaps. The week after, at the latest." He leaves me standing at the gate. I look around to find that I am completely alone – even Moloch has disappeared. I must go in.

As I pass a storeroom, I feel myself grabbed from behind, and I hear a voice in my ear, hissing, "You don't know how long I have been waiting for the moment when you were alone!"

It's Cut-hand's voice, and there's his mate now, grabbing my legs, trying to get a rope round me. I do not waste my time trying to scream – firstly it's not my style, and secondly it's a waste of energy – but I begin to laugh again. I have just spent my valuable breath talking about a dead time when my uncle and cousins routinely tried to molest me, and here is more of the same happening! I begin to pump my legs up and down, right-left, right-left, to make it difficult for the thug who is trying to grapple with them. I push backwards against Cut-hand, and start to think of effective ways to get out of this. I am not the comparative weakling I was the day I scratched his paw for him.

Suddenly there is a thud, and a grunt. Cut-hand's grip loosens, and he falls backwards. His mate is backing away, with fear in his eyes. I roll free, and jump up. Moloch is advancing on him, arms outstretched.

I surprise him by slapping one of his arms down. He looks at me.

"I can take care of myself!" I yell. I turn my back and walk off. I remember the Lanista's warning to me, about laying a hand on one of his people – and I don't care. My cheeks, ears, and neck are on fire.

CHAPTER XI

The next time I came to the dig, after our visits to the Colosseum and the Trevi Fountain, I was surprised not to find Vittorio. I couldn't see his familiar overalls anywhere, and I felt let down. You must understand that the one day at the dig and the one day sight-seeing had quickly become very important to me, giving a framework to the week, which made me want to keep going.

When the sky threatened to turn black again, the thought that the next day or the day after would mean that I was here or somewhere else in the transformed city with Vittorio, steadied me, and made things bearable. So to be here at the dig, and not to see him, was like having a treat spoiled.

No one volunteered any information about him, and I got on with my sieving. The work seemed slow and boring. The volunteers and the professional archaeologists knelt in their trenches, like a colony of beetles, gently scratching at the ground. Even Signor Ciani kept himself very busy, and was uncommunicative during his breaks for coffee or for lunch. There were few finds of any note, certainly nothing like the medallion.

But for the beetling and scratching, the dig might as well have stopped, and the bulldozers moved in.

It was mid-afternoon when I finally caught sight of Vittorio. I should say that what I actually caught sight of was the familiar set of overalls a hundred metres away, maybe a hundred and fifty. I had been vaguely aware of a black car slowing and stopping on the road that led to the dig. It was big, and it was low. With tinted windows, making it impossible to see inside, it was a car that, well, looked like it meant business – and that business was none of mine, it seemed to say, because it had stopped at that discreet distance. A rear door opened, catching the sun's light and reflecting it, and it was this sudden flash that made me deliberately look at it. Vittorio got out. I put down my sieve, rubbed the soil from my hands, and started to walk towards the car. Then I noticed that two or three of the beetling diggers had also seen the car, and had actually turned their heads towards me, as if to see what I would do. I didn't like this. I checked my step, and looked for some activity to do, to explain my movement in that direction. Finding none, I went down rather awkwardly on one knee and re-tied my bootlaces, trying to make it look as though I was not still watching the car.

Another man got out of the car. I could see that he

was wearing a dark suit, a white shirt, and a sober tie. I had the silly idea that he had borrowed his outfit from Vittorio. It was almost like a uniform. The other man had an attaché case, which he unzipped, taking some papers out of it. I could see him talking to Vittorio, looking attentively at him. Vittorio took the papers from his hand and read them, nodding occasionally as the other man spoke. A pause seemed to follow, and then Vittorio, accepting a pen from the other man, signed the papers and handed them back to him.

After a further exchange of words, Vittorio extended a hand. I expected the other man to grip it in a handshake, but – here I stopped even pretending to tie my bootlaces – he took it almost delicately, bowed, and kissed it!

Vittorio turned and started to walk towards the site. The other man got back into the car, which made a U-turn and sped off towards the city. I stood up and went back to my sieve, my face on fire. Thank heaven all the beetles had their heads down again, and could not see me. My heart seemed to bang against my ribs. What sort of man – a man of influence, a man of connections, a man who was addressed as 'Boss' – gets out of a black car, and has his hand kissed by a suited minion? No wonder he had this air of authority. No wonder crowds seemed to part for him. No wonder he could get us into places. It hadn't been my imagination after all. I had indeed been walking down the streets with a leopard on a chain, and the chain had been round *my* neck.

I was furious. I don't know whether my fury was directed at Vittorio, or at my stupid self. How could I fall for a man like that – a man of his type? I had seen every kind of low-life back in the country from which I had escaped, and now here I was in Rome, and I had been taken in! For the rest of the afternoon I worked with my sieve like a robot. I washed finds on auto-pilot. I took some ribbing from a couple of volunteers, who said I was washing away the patina of centuries, and ought to go and wash dishes in a trattoria. If anyone had seen me pretending to tie my bootlaces, no one mentioned the fact. No one said a word to me about Vittorio, who spent the rest of the day in conversation with Signor Ciani.

At the end of the day, I accepted a taxi ride back to my apartment. For the first half of the journey we said nothing, and I wished to keep it that way, but we got caught in traffic, and Vittorio broke the silence.

"I'm sorry I was late today," he said. I shrugged my shoulders.

"I had business," he went on.

I wanted to say, "Yes, I noticed." But I said nothing.

I didn't even look at him. There was another silence, broken only by car horns, excited shouts from outside, and some muttered curses from the taxi driver. Again Vittorio spoke. I was aware that he was looking at me, but I stared ahead, half-hating him.

"I have to go away," he said. "On business. I will be away a week. Maybe longer – a fortnight. Maybe three weeks. I can't really say."

No reaction from me. The traffic was moving again, the taxi driver had stopped cursing, and was now whistling to himself, as if trying to block out our one-sided conversation, aware that he shouldn't be listening. We were getting near the Via Stoccolma.

"Are you all right?"

"I'm fine," I said. "I'm fine, Don Vittorio."

I had laid a slight emphasis on the "Don". That was unnecessary of course, as the very presence of that word said everything. It said, "I know." It said, "How could you deceive me?" It said, "If you think I care, you're wrong!" It said, "Do you think I'm shocked? The only difference between you and our local librarian ordering his squad of camouflaged swaggerers around is money, and a midnight-blue suit!" It said, "Who did you think I was talking about, when you came into my space, sat me on the sofa, made me a cup of tea, and made me cry?" It said everything I wanted to say to him, short of actually saying it. It said a few other things which I didn't want to say to him, and which I didn't want to admit. It said, "I'm a complete fool, but it's all over now." It said, "The moment of quiet and the legion of ghosts in the Colosseum, and the gaiety and the splash of sunlight on the spray of the Trevi fountain – they're torn up, gone, forgotten, worthless, tainted, as unwelcome in my mind now as the memories of ruined, darkened streets in Srebrenice. You did that to me. *You* did that to me."

When the taxi pulled up in Via Stoccolma I got out, and went determinedly to the driver's window.

"I'll pay the fare to here," I said, daring Vittorio to argue about it. He said nothing. I went inside – my turn to leave him without a backward glance.

CHAPTER XII

"Patricius," I say, now that we have tired of today's game, "You have been coming here for about six months now, and I still don't know why you came that first time."

"No more do I. I have often wondered. Look, gladiatorial combat is supposed to serve the purpose of strengthening the Roman character, and making us accept the need for struggle and death to maintain our greatness. That's the theory. In practice people come out of a sort of blood-lust. Or else out of social necessity, and that is the reason I go to the games – as little as possible up until recently, I might add, only when it's, well, socially necessary. I have been a soldier. I have seen real bloodshed. I know about the martial virtues we Romans are supposed to have. I have seen it. I have seen an advancing line waver, and then continue at the double because its standard-bearer ran forward. I have seen one man tackle several enemies at once, for no reason that was apparent, but just out of bloody-mindedness it seemed. I have seen men stand for hours in the cold, in their lines, waiting to go into battle, only to be turned round and dismissed. I have seen a soldier run between watchtowers on the frontier, just to deliver a message, because the beacon was too wet to light. I have seen soldiers fighting to the last, not flinching until they were cut down. I have seen this not just in our own legions, but in the enemy too, even in the midst of a disorganised, barbarian rabble. Oh sure, I've seen stupidity, and failure, and cowardice – today's coward becomes tomorrow's hero, and vice versa – and sometimes I feel that there is nothing more stupid in the whole world than the glory of Rome. Maybe dying for it is."

He pauses for breath. "Go on," I say.

"The first time I ever saw you fight was the day of your first kill."

Oh yes, I remember that one. A net-man. I spent ten minutes dodging cast after cast of that net, looking for some way inside its reach that wouldn't end up with me totally entangled. Then my shield-arm got caught, but not cleanly, and I began to wind the net around my arm – he was too stupid to let go, and all I had to watch out for was his trident. I remember parrying it outside, and stepping forward. Then I trapped the shaft under my arm, and we began to struggle for it, but I was working my way forward along the shaft, holding my sword out towards his belly, and I was getting closer. Then he lost his nerve, and dropped his end of the net and the trident, and ran. I chased after him, and at first the crowd laughed, but then they got angry to see such cowardice.

"When he began to tire, you skimmed your shield at him, like a discus. I think he was too flabbergasted to move. It was ingenious – knocked him flat. Even I was on my feet. The crowd, and the President – I think it was the Emperor that day – were in no mood to spare him. I recall the signal for death being given, and wondering whether I was the only person for whom it was a sombre moment."

"Yes, it was the Emperor himself that day," I say. And then, "Do you know something, I don't think he even watches what's going on most of the time. He sits in earnest discussion – or idle chat, I don't know – with someone else up on the tribunal. I've seen him – when I used to sit in the sunny seats. Hmmm. It was a sombre moment for me too. But it was my destiny to kill the net-man. I was awake all night afterwards, but I did it. I have never lost any sleep since then."

Patricius says, "Oh he watches you, Eunice. Any halfway decent Emperor makes a point of watching someone whose fame is growing, even a slave. No offence meant. Can he use this person to his own ends? Is this person dangerous? He watched the kill very keenly, and you carried it out like a professional slaughterman. The net-man went out like a candle. I was there the first time you actually killed in combat, too."

"No offence taken. I *am* a slave. I remember the first time I was called that, and by whom, and under what circumstances. I had a few more butcherings of defeated opponents to do before I actually killed someone who was still holding his sword. A veteran from the barracks across the city. He was talking to me for the first few minutes – how he had come to knock me off my perch, how he was sick of hearing my name, how I was a whore, what he was going to do to me once he had cut the straps to my cuirass, how he was going back to the barracks that night as the man who killed Lupa, how the crowd was going to be shouting his name. I can't even remember it, myself. He knew all the wrong things to say to me, and pretty soon he stopped talking, because we were hammering each other for all we were worth. I was down, then I was up. He was down, then he was up. I'll never forget his clenched teeth. We used everything we could, knees and elbows when we got too close to stab or slash. Honestly, Patricius, now I look back, I think it could have gone either way, and I might not have been here with you now. But somehow, I got inside his guard and opened him up. It must have hurt, but he kept on coming at me. The more he came at me, the more I cut him. The more I cut him, the weaker he got. And all the time, since that first cut, he growled through those clenched teeth, and growled, and growled. He kept on coming and he kept on growling. Eventually he was coming for me on his hands and knees, flailing feebly with his sword. He was mad!"

As I pause, Patricius says nothing ~~for a while~~ for a while, then, "No, I don't think it was madness."

"What else could it have been? I stood back for a moment, and he got up. He was bleeding everywhere, coughing up blood, but still growling. He staggered forward, and I took him with the point of my sword, right under his left ear. It went right into his brain, but he staggered on for about six paces, and it was wrenched right out of my hand. It was only then that I realised that I had some bad cuts too. I was almost too exhausted to walk back out of the arena."

"But you did."

"But I did," I say. "You said you didn't think it was madness. What was it, then?"

"Look, I said I had been in battle, and seen the best and the worst in men who fight for a living. I have been initiated into the soldier's mystery, which is not for a woman to know. But that man you defeated and killed had something in common with you, and I saw it in both of you, and that must be why I have come again and again – more often than social necessity would dictate – to see you fight. Yes, it's why I come here too. We have two words that describe it badly: virtue and duty. But they won't do. Like everything we have copied from the Greeks, we have made a crude copy only. We think that, because our Empire contains Greece, we are better than the Greeks, but that thought is the pinnacle of our philosophy. The Greeks call these things *arete* and *ergon*. The first, I guess, holds in its meaning something of one's nature, one's role in life, one's place in creation, the perfect template to which one must aspire, the adult state towards which one must grow. The second, well, what one must do, what one cannot avoid doing, what there is no question of not doing, in order to fulfil the first. For all his hate and anger, that man who kept on coming and kept on growling could do no less. You too, are a person with a keen sense of her *arete*, and *ergon*. That is why I come to see you. I have never seen this so clearly in any man or woman. I want to be near this wonderful thing. Never lose sight of this, Eunice."

I say, "What do you mean by the soldier's mystery?"

He makes no answer to this, but stands up, and reaches into a pouch at his waist. "Take this little keepsake," he says, and hands me a small, silver disc. It has a hole for a thong or chain. There is writing stamped on one side, and a crescent moon, the sign of Diana, on the face. While I am looking at it, he leaves.

I take it back to my room. I sit here for hours, looking at it. I miss dinner.

When I was a girl, Diana was my favourite deity. I would make a little nightly ritual to her. Later in my life outside this place I would follow it up with a few words to Hecate, on the subject of my uncle and cousins. I had thought about neither goddess since I arrived here. My way had led me inexorably into the kingdom of Nemesis – unavoidable fate and doom – who had to be placated without fail. Only once had I failed to do so, and my survival at that time seemed to be a period of grace I had used up. I would only be handed over to another god when Nemesis had done with me, and that would be to one who had sailed here from Egypt to be close to death, because he is the lord of death, so Croc told me: Anubis, with the jackal's head, gatekeeper to and ruler of a gladiator's final destination.

The writing on Patricius' gift is some line of poetry; I am not interested in it. But this crescent moon seems to speak to me. I sit looking at it until a shaft of real moonlight shines through my window, and with it comes inspiration from the goddess herself. I turn the medallion around so that her sign lays upon its back, and then I see what was hidden to me before. The points of the crescent are like two upraised horns!

Patricius may well have been referring to a simple brotherhood of soldiers, but I am sure now that there was a deeper meaning to what he said – perhaps he did not realise what he was saying to me. He is, I am sure, a follower of the cult of Mithras, the bull-slayer. I know nothing about this craft, but now my mind seems to burn with a curiosity that is close to divine madness. I lie on my bed. I can't sleep – for the first time since my first kill.

CHAPTER XIII

Don't imagine that I wasted any tears when I got into my flat. I shut the door, and put my back against it, as if to say that a period in my life was over. Another period in my life. Another milestone of impermanence.

I gave up going to the internet café. The last time I was there my latte went cold, and I sat for half an hour staring at a search engine without putting anything in it. A waste of money, an expensive way to consume coffee. I can only say that I rattled around, either on the local street or in the flat. I hardly ever went into the centre of Rome, and instead I wore a groove in the pavement between the flat and the nearest general store. I developed a liking for green bananas and motoring magazines. I have no idea why.

One day I did try to break out of this, and headed for the city centre. Impossible, even on the *Linea B*, even after rush hour. Some foreign dignitary was on a state visit to Italy. There were crowds everywhere, there were police, there were groups of protesters, there were delays and obstructions, there were confrontations, there was no point in persisting. I gave up. Perhaps I would go tomorrow. Perhaps I would go next week. Perhaps not.

Perhaps I would take a coach trip to Ravenna, use up more of my savings, and force myself to find something to do – gainful employment.

Arriving back from that futile attempt, I found that the phone was ringing. The answering machine had just kicked in as I reached for the receiver, and I heard Vittorio's voice. I almost ignored this; it seemed to be an intrusion from something – someone – that I had left behind, and from which I had moved on. My first impulse was to press the button on the answering machine that took the volume down, and in fact I kidded myself that I was reaching over to do that, but my hand came back holding the receiver.

"Ignore the machine. I'm here. What do you want?"

"Jelena, I have a couple of surprises for you. May I come round?"

"Are these surprises any better than the last one?"

He went quiet at the other end of the line, then he said, "I can explain. Really, that's what one of the surprises is all about. May I come round? Say, in an hour's time? Is that convenient?"

"Yes," I said, and hung up.

Did I agree against my better judgment? I can't tell. Just at that moment I didn't really care whether he did come. Come or stay away, it was all the same to me.

Nevertheless, I suddenly realised that I had changed, and combed my hair, and that I was scurrying around the flat getting things straight, and I cursed myself. Damn biology!

CHAPTER XIV

It is the dead of night – starless, and with a chilly breeze. I wrap my cloak around me, and pull up the hood. I am standing alone, outside the gate. Yes, outside!

A few nights ago, something had disturbed me - I am sleeping only fitfully at present – and I slipped out of my room and through the sleeping barracks, in time to see one of the other gladiators run silently across the yard. He ducked into the shadows by the gatepost, where he seemed to be waiting, maybe watching. In my own patch of shadow I stayed as motionless as I could, not knowing whether to go up and ask him what he was up to, or to stay there and see what happened next. I was getting a cramp in one foot, and was on the point of stepping out into the middle of the yard, when he emerged from the shadow. He had taken off his sandals, and hung them around his neck. He grasped two of the vertical iron bars of the gate and, pushing backwards, placed one of his bare feet against them. Then he began to climb, getting as much traction as he could from bare hands and feet, using the crossbars as momentary resting places. Surprisingly quickly he reached the top, clambered gingerly over the spikes, slid halfway down the other side, and then jumped. He landed almost noiselessly, with knees bent, and darted into the shadows on that side. After a further minute or so, during which time he must have put his sandals on again, I saw him run swiftly up the street and round a corner.

I stayed there almost the whole night. It must have been about an hour before dawn when I saw him return and cautiously climb back over the gate. This time, as he crossed back towards the barracks building, I stepped out into his way. He stopped, with a sharp intake of breath, and we stood looking at each other. We said nothing. I didn't ask him what his errand or assignation had been, I just kept on looking at him. Then I turned and walked in. I didn't bother to look back to see whether he was following me, I simply went back to my room. I sat on my bed, and watched through my window as the sky softened into morning and the swallows came out to scream at one another.

No one amongst the other gladiators meets my eyes often, except perhaps Moloch, but now one of them avoids looking at me at all costs. He is still afraid that I have something on him. It will be, perhaps, several weeks before he realises that I don't care. Meanwhile, I still don't care; I don't care if he is nervous or resentful –

I have other things on my mind.

Today I was expecting a visit from Patricius. It is his usual day, but he didn't come. I paced the yard, I cast anxious glances up the street. I hung around until it was time to go in. No show. But I needed to talk to him – I need desperately to talk to him. I have to ask him again, "What is the soldier's mystery?" and to press him for an answer and an explanation. Why? I don't know. I have never felt such a compulsion. Maybe this is something I have to do in order to be who I am. Maybe it is because it is forbidden to women, and I am more than just a woman. Maybe it is because he has let that little piece of information slip, and I can't resist going for a weakness. What am I prepared to do to find out more? What would I do to force him? What would I do to persuade him? What price would I be prepared to pay?

He didn't come.

That is why, having lain until well past midnight until I could hear no sound, I got up, left my room, and came out into the yard. Just as I had seen it done, I climbed the gate with my sandals round my neck, and jumped down on the other side. Now I am standing here stupidly.

Into the shadows, fool!

This is the start of something. I am back – near enough – where I was all those years ago, when I first came to this place. So many Rubicons crossed – another just now. Now, for the first time in years, another chance to turn and go back. Deliberately, I put my sandals on; being shod again will mean I am more likely to go on. I stand, and count to fifty. There is a gust, and it seems like a spirit hand giving me a push. And so I am off!

I sprint round the corner and stop. My heart is banging. No sounds of pursuit. I go on. I make my way through the streets, although there is barely enough light to see – a few guttering torches, the occasional lamp still burning behind a curtain, a watchman's brazier, no more than a moment of moonlight through a gap in the clouds, mostly I make out shapes that are less totally dark than other shapes and bless our city-builders for thinking in straight lines. For a while I am in streets I have either passed down during our processions to the amphitheatre, or have seen on the way, and I am fairly sure where I am going. Now I am in streets I only remember from the days before I was Lupa. Now not even those. But I have guessed where Patricius' house must be, from the things he has told me during our conversations, and I am dogged in my heading for it, though I have to back-track twice out of dead-ends.

How long have I been in these streets? I have strolled as nonchalantly as possible past the occasional group of people coming home late. Once I hid until a couple of off-duty soldiers had passed me. Now, am I here? Have I arrived? I want to see before me a plain wall, about half as tall again as a man, a portico, a door with an alcove on either side in which lanterns are lit – that will fit the description of the rear entrance to Patricius' house. I see it, and I pause in the shadow. Tonight's journey has been one of light-shadow, light-shadow, shadow, shadow, shadow...

What now? Shall I knock on the door? No, it's opening, and someone's coming out. It's a man, in a hooded cloak not unlike mine. By his bearing, it must be Patricius. He looks from left to right, as if to check whether he is observed, and then sets off away from me. That's him all right, I recognise his stride, and I start forward, about to call him or run and catch him, but something checks me and makes me follow him – light-shadow, light-shadow – at a distance. Where is he going at this time of night? This time of night – ha! I came expecting him to be awake, didn't I. I don't know what I really was expecting. I don't know what I am expecting now. And I don't know where I am going, he is leading me by a zig-zag route, down alleyways I don't recognise, into areas of the city I would not expect him to frequent. (What am I saying? I wouldn't expect him to frequent the gates of our barracks!)

What now? I think I have lost him! There are three alleys here – which one has he taken? Listen. Can I hear footsteps? No, only my own pulse in my ears. The right-hand alley, then. No, the left, I'll go down the left. Quick, quick. Round a sharp angle of a building, past thorn bushes, following a crumbling wall...yes! That's him, further ahead but it is, it is. He is turning, and going behind...what? Run up to the place, stumbling – careful! Quiet! I can see nothing.

Wait. What is this – a door? The mouth of a cave? Deeper darkness in the darkness, but like a wild beast's eye there is a glimmer of red deep inside. A torch? Yes. In – follow, hands reaching out and to the side, sometimes upwards to gauge the height of the passage. It's lighter now, with side passages hewn out of rock, and torches in some of them. A catacomb. Some figures are moving through them, but always down. A cloaked man is walking ahead of me. It is not Patricius. Another is walking behind me, not him either, but where have they come from? Where are they going? Down, down, until we reach a chamber, into which all the passages seem to flow, and every cloaked, hooded figure stops. I flatten myself against a wall, and risk a look around. A few more arrive. Ah – there he is now, coming in by that other passage! He stops. He turns his head over to my side of the chamber. His face is in shadow, and mine surely must be, but for a few moments it seems he is looking right at me. Then he turns to face in the direction everyone else is facing, and I do the same.

Many of the torches have been put out now. Most of the light is coming from a fire, which glows red on the other side of the chamber. There is yet another hooded man over by it. He throws something onto the fire, and the flames leap up, flooding the chamber with a golden light, and I see that between him and us is a life-size statue – an idol – of a bull. I am in the Mithraeum!

The priest, as I guess him to be, throws back his hood. He is a tall, broad-shouldered man, with a mane of hair like an old likeness of Alexander the Great. The glow of the fire begins to subside; he takes a cup and pours some liquid over the bull's head. A libation. I am watching something forbidden to women, a ritual of the soldier's mystery! There is a scent in the air – sharp like cinnamon, heady like wild flowers. The firelight softens to orange, and my eyes are somehow fixed to the silhouette of the priest, cup upraised. But it is as if the bull is stirring, breathing, and in the priest's hand is no cup but a sword, which he is plunging down into the bull's neck. There is a convulsion – I can't tear my eyes away – man and bull shiver and shake and fall. The glow from the fire is now dull red, and there is a shapeless mass in front of it, black, horrible. It rises, it forms, it holds my eye, and I know a numbing fear that I have never known before, because the silhouette I now see is like nothing so much as that terrible beast that haunted the labyrinth, rending its victims limb from limb – the Minotaur of legend! How it grows! How it advances on me! Am I going mad?

Suddenly I am running, out of the chamber and back up the passages, brushing past the hooded figures, hardly knowing which way to run. I have some vague feeling I must follow the torches, but there are so many passages. When I come to a fork or a four-ways I falter; but when I look back the way I have come, there seems to be a shadow growing on the wall, coming nearer, vast and horned. So on and on in near-panic, holding on desperately to some sanity, hoping, sobbing, panting prayers to whichever god can hear me. And suddenly out into fresh air, through the opening. Am I safe? I look back, and see the red eye of the first torch wink out into blackness, and I know only too well what nightmare shape has obscured it. Run! Run!

Run! Old wall – thorns – sharp angle – run! Alleyways – left – right – which? Run! Knocking into things in the dark – sending things clattering and rolling – alleyways – right – left – run! Always behind me, appearing at every corner passed, a shadow, horns – run! Fear, fear, fear – what is piercing my side and stinging my eyes? Run! Narrow streets – broad streets – streets I almost recognise – but made hellish and unreal by that shadow, always looming round the last corner – run!

Suddenly I blunder into the bars of the gate, and without taking off my sandals I scramble up and over, tearing skin and cloak in the process. I risk one look back, and still that horned shadow looms larger and larger. How can even the bars of this gate stop it? Somehow I make it to my room, slam the door, and lean my back hard against it, panting, sobbing. There are noises in the barracks now. Grunts, queries – who's making that noise? Who's waking us up? What's going on? Shut up! But I am past caring about that.

O Nemesis! Is this my inevitable doom? Will I ever sleep again? I feel something hard and painful in my hand. Digging into my flesh is the silver disk. There is blood on the horns of the moon.

Patricius – what have I done?

CHAPTER XV

Vittorio's knock is usually firm and definite. There was a hesitancy about it on this occasion. I stopped straightening cushions and stood up.

"It's not locked," I called. "You know I don't lock it."

The door opened. In walked a Roman Catholic Monsignor. He had at the same time the dignity of a cardinal and yet an apologetic step. He was tall. He wore a black, clerical robe down to his feet. A silver crucifix hung on a chain around his neck. The only other thing about him which was not black was the white of his clerical collar. His hair was dark and had a wave in it; the lenses of his sunglasses seemed as black as everything else. There was a wry smile on his lips, and a sudden wave of recognition swept over me, as he took off the sunglasses to reveal eyes that twinkled with diabolically attractive mischief. Vittorio. Don Vittorio! *Don* Vittorio!

I was blazing mad. At myself primarily, for having a crush on a Catholic priest, like those who had fuelled hatred for Serbs like me, a representative of this monstrous city in which I was now hopelessly trapped. At him for letting me think he was a high-ranking mobster, and for leading me on, letting me have this crush on him. His eyes seemed to me to be saying, "Do you really think you are the first woman to find me attractive? Or to find any priest attractive?"

"You sod!" I exclaimed, advancing on him, looking for something to throw.

He held up his hand. "The next surprise, Jelena! The next surprise, then you can hit me!" he said. "There's someone else here you ought to meet."

He took a couple of steps back to the door, and beckoned to someone who was obviously waiting outside. A young man walked in, rather tentatively, looking round as if to take stock of his surroundings. He was dressed in one of Vittorio's suits, but he didn't fill it as well as its owner did, so it looked ill-fitting and a little baggy on him. He looked at me, and there was a flicker of uncertain recognition in his eyes. I just stood there, and my brain refused to work. How many more surprises could I possibly cope with? This seemed to be one too far, and I guess I must have gone into total denial. I didn't recognise him. I couldn't recognise him. I refused to recognise him, and I saw disappointment in his eyes. He was talking to me, words, words, words I wouldn't understand. He stopped talking, looked at Vittorio, and shrugged. Vittorio gave him a nod of encouragement, and he spoke again.

"Jelena, it's me," he said, and I realised that my brain had been refusing to register Serbo-Croat.

By the time I had left the country of my birth, the country of my birth no longer existed. My native language no longer existed. Serbs spoke Serbian, and Croats spoke Croatian, each damned tribe accentuating the slight differences, until these differences became a political badge, a sign of ethnic purity.

Stubbornly, Franjo and I had stuck to the old, official Creole of Jugoslavia. It was our gesture of defiance, until such time as we really understood that defiance would get us killed, staying together would get us killed, one wrong word would get us killed. We had, each in our own way, chosen to live. How long ago was it? How many milestones of impermanence had I passed since then? It was impossible to take any backward step; but then, what was backwards, and what was forwards, if nothing was real? Surely it would not hurt me to recognise the young man, as he had certainly recognised me. He needed a haircut, and a shave. He needed a shower and a good meal. In fact he needed feeding and looking after in general. He needed to get out of that suit, and into a pair of jeans. He needed to lose a few years. He needed to lose the haunted, fearful look in his eyes in the days before he had gone away with the men who knew where his family lived in Dubrovnik. He needed to become a young, optimistic graduate, getting a job in Srebrenice. I needed to become a young, optimistic girl, with a family. Then I could recognise him – I could recognise him easily. But the world would just not stand still and let me do this. Every time I tried to grab hold of something solid and permanent, the world turned upside down again, again, again.

But while all this refusal, all this impossibility, all this impermanence, while all these things had been whirling in my head, one of us, or both of us, had crossed the huge gulf that was the two or three steps distance between, across the room. I knew this must have happened, because we were holding each other, and I *was* recognising, *had* recognised him. I remembered precisely how much taller than me he was, and the angle I had to make with my elbow to crook my arm round him and rest a hand below his shoulder blade. I remembered precisely how deeply he breathed, and the pace of those breaths. I remembered the rhythm of his heart against his ribs. I remembered how our contours matched if we stood exactly so. And despite everything, I remembered him, and I could no longer refuse to recognise him. As we held each other now, I sobbed.

This wasn't like the last time I had been in tears at the flat, after that day of blackness, when Vittorio had found me, and I had ranted incoherently about Rome. My sobs now were tearless, great gulps coming from deep down inside me, gasps for air as if I was drowning. No one listening could have told that each sob was an attempt to say the name of the man I was holding.

Why is it that the normal impulse at times like this appears to be for someone to make a hot drink? On this occasion I needed to do it. Three cups of instant coffee suddenly had a sharper reality for me than all that had happened in the few minutes since two incongruously dressed men had walked into the flat. So I pulled myself together, turned a sob into a deep breath, and pushed myself free of Franjo's embrace. I held him at arm's length and smiled. He was grinning with relief by now. I guess for him to be here in Italy, in a place where he didn't understand the language – he had never done it at school – being conducted, by a cleric, to meet a young woman at a flat in a strange city, was as unsettling an experience as anything I had recently been through. It's all relative.

So I bustled in the kitchen, clattered mugs around, opened and closed drawers, jars, and the refrigerator, until I had rattled and clattered myself into a state of relative equilibrium. I took a tray with three mugs and an unopened box of *biscotti* into the lounge, and settled the three of us into a half-comfortable triangle on the edges of the sofa and an armchair.

Vittorio had a look on his face I had never seen before. It struck me that he too was vulnerable. All that had happened had brought him down to earth, locked up the fictional mobster, caged the leopard, even defrocked the priest, made him wonderfully ordinary, made him my friend. He was moved, I could tell. He held yet another handkerchief tightly, and made no move to pass it to me. Franjo looked from me to him, and from him to me, as we talked in Italian. Poor Franjo, so recently found, must have felt ignored, even though he was the subject of our conversation.

"He's the reason I went away," said Vittorio. "I couldn't tell you what I was doing, in case it all went wrong."

"Just then, believing what I did, I wouldn't have cared anyhow. I wouldn't have listened."

"I know, I know. But it could have gone very wrong. It's usually an advantage being part of a worldwide organisation like the Catholic Church. It can open so many doors. But some of them can easily slam shut in your face. I could count on the help of most of the hierarchy in Croatia, but there was only so much I could tell them. Imagine trying to tell someone that you wanted to trace someone who may have been in a Croat Militia squad, and you wanted to take him out of the country, and you were doing this on behalf of a Serbian woman. The explanation may have been innocent and true, but not many people would have believed it. So I had to hold half the story back, and that was dangerous in its own way. People will read into the gaps what they want to read, and – bang – another door slams.

"Eventually I found him in Split, not Dubrovnik. Oh Jelena, don't ask him about his family – let him tell you in his own time. And don't ask him how many Serbs they made him kill. He will have to live with that. I can't say anything more – I heard his confession."

"I have been through enough to know how fragile the past is," I said. "And what's more, I know how difficult it is to forget things. I'll try, I promise."

That was a promise that went far beyond mere words. I had no idea whether I could keep it.

CHAPTER XVI

I have spent much of my waiting time looking at a pen containing a bull. We have had bull-leaping as one of the preliminary acts in this Games – the Emperor wished to give us a history lesson, it seemed. I stared for a long time into the bull's eyes, daring it to be more than a bull. But it remained only a bull.

The whole barracks has been as silent as a stone for two days. Except for the swallows. Two days ago we were told what was planned for today's games. It was something that does not happen often at the top outfits in Rome – at the meat-yards in Iberia or Egypt maybe – but word got out that two fighters from this place would be going up against each other. Money may not smell, but sometimes it talks persuasively, and it takes a top Lanista to persuade to the contrary. Power talks even more persuasively, however, and this time the persuasion came right from the top. Two fighters from this place are indeed going up against each other – two unbeaten champions – at Caesar's request. If there is a particular reason for this request, you can be sure it won't filter down this far. We shall never know.

Since I went outside that night, my waking hours have

been plagued by a demon that sits on my shoulder, making me snap and spit at everyone, batter practice dummies to pieces, bruise and wind my sparring partners, blunt and break swords. Pass-water is passing fire, so they say. But better by far to be plagued in the daytime by a demon I can curse at and run ragged with hard work, than to be plagued at night by one I can't. Sometimes I have managed to sleep; more often than not dreams are blood red, with a growing, lowering, black shape, and end in violent awakening and sweat. Sometimes I thought I was poisoned, and even my wine ration, sweetened by honey, in a leaden cup can't dull the fear. Only by concentrating on the Games, on the prospect of getting out into the arena, did I make that night-vision lurk a little further behind me, and kept his byre-stinking breath from my neck. Today – like I said – at Caesar's request, two unbeaten champions are going up against each other.

Moloch and I.

Patricius has not been to see me. As we marched from the barracks to the Colosseum, I occasionally looked at the gawping *polloi* lining the street, to see if he was there, but gave up on that after only a short while. Most of the time, looking grimly ahead, I just marched. I heard a few remarks and shouts – an encouragement, a ribald comment, a commendation to Fortuna – but I did not turn my head. Only Moloch and I did not march in the ranks of five. We walked separately, each followed by an armour-bearer. I was aware, from what I could see out of the corner of my eye, that Moloch was sullen. He made none of his usual threatening gestures, but strode along as silently as I did. The march seemed to take forever, but once the doors of the amphitheatre shut behind us, I feel as though I had only just stepped out of our gates. I laugh at this little quirk of time and mind.

My name has been called, and so I walk up the tunnel. Moloch is already at the top. I pause only to make a cursory obeisance to Nemesis, and set off to join him there. Even though I know that he never prays to Nemesis – if he says a prayer to one of his outlandish demons I do not know – it seems to me that he is in a hurry to get outside into the arena. So I slow down, and walk deliberately up to the gate, checking and adjusting my gear as I go. Only when I am quite composed do I half turn my head and look at him, or rather at his hideous helmet. He does the same.

Now I realise something. Or – no – I knew it all the time and would not admit it. This will not be one of those duels where there is a chance of both of us walking away at the end. It will be something where Rome will show its power of life and death over us. It will be an objective lesson, to those watching, in the fact of life-and-death struggle. Either they will see Rome overcome the mighty Barbarian, or they will see what happens when she allows herself to weaken and fall into the outer darkness. This is to be a deciding match of champions, and they will see something, even if it is we two impaled on each other's sword, bleeding our last. Moloch knows this too.

Gates open. Out into the sunshine. I look about, as if this is my first time, or my last – the cheap seats, the tribunal, I wonder if Patricius is here? We stop. We raise our swords. Hail, Caesar.

I am aware of my whole body, of a slight ache in my left calf, of a certain light-headedness, of the weight of my armour. I hunch and relax my shoulders.

Moloch, will you dance with me?

There's a thought which almost makes me laugh, and I have done no more of that since I found myself in that Tartarus, that unclean hole, that blasphemy. But this is the zenith of one life, here in this universe of sand, with chaos outside it, this great, yellow disc as hot as the sun above. One of us, who stands at the alert, waiting for the cries to die down, will ride with Phoebus, and the other will crash with Icarus.

There – is that enough silence for you? My fans have stopped howling for me, because I willed them to stop. All eyes are on me, because I willed them to be on me, even the Emperor's. You are all here because I brought you here. I am here, because I willed it, all those years ago. Step after forward step I have taken; step after step you have all taken with me. Nothing could have stopped it. Nothing could have changed it. Nemesis. All that you are, you are because of me. All that I am, even though I am a slave, I am by my own will. If I called out to you to run wild and destroy the whole city, you would do it for me. I hold you in my hand!

But, we who are about to die salute you.

Patricius. I wonder if you are in the audience.

*

Because it is just that: a dance.

The fighting routines that we learn, that we spend so much time forcing our bodies to follow, so that they are no stranger to us than breathing, have something of the formal, the ritualistic about them. We are down here on the sand telling Rome a story about itself that it wants to hear. Rome is about bravery. Rome is about fighting. Rome is about being prepared to face – or watch – death.

Moloch and I face each other in the sun, identically armed with sword and targe, identically armoured with helmet, breastplate and greaves. Only his size and my shape make it plain who we are. Between us, the arbiter holds his staff high. Only his eyes are on the tribunal – ours are flickering lights, barely seen beneath our visors, but we know that I am staring at Moloch, and he is staring at me. Once the arbiter drops his staff and steps back, that will be the beginning of the end game. The fox will chase the geese, the geese will peck the fox, until one is dinner for the other. Mad, mad, mad! No one will step forward to separate us this time – we will only be separated by the Styx.

A gasp is the only hint that a signal has been given from above. A split second later staff and arbiter are out of our field of vision. Let us give them a show, we two creatures out of legend, one a child-eating beast, one an unnatural amazon. First they will appreciate some stalking, so we prowl around each other in a circle, letting the tension build up almost to the point where some of the crowd despair of their being any action. Even I am impatient, for I am the one who makes the first move. I make it look as though I have thrown caution aside, and dash into the attack.

The crowd begins to roar.

Moloch is no novice, and meets my attack with parries as tense and resilient as bowstrings. As we spring apart again, the roar becomes a steady buzz of excitement. And now the dance begins. If it is not precisely choreographed, it is at least made up of move and counter-move, strung together in combinations we have both seen scores of times before. One of us appears to press forward as the other falls back, then the roles are reversed.

So: right foot forward, feint a jab, rotate the wrist and change to a cut to the head which is deflected by his shield. Catch a cut to my waist with my own shield, and step in with the left, swinging my sword underarm, upwards from hip to shoulder. Parried. Backhand slash, both together, momentarily caught hilt-to-hilt, then break free. Clash shields and barge, break free again. Wide, swinging blows aimed at the neck and chest. Good stuff – faster than they've seen before – and hard work. Mouth slightly open, breathing easily, but beginning to sweat. Duck a cut to the head, and press on inside the follow-through, spin round and backhand slash – applause, as it bounces off his shield with a loud thump. Now his turn: right foot, lunge parried, up-and-down three times our swords clatter together. Move back, change guard, left foot leading, deflect several body-cuts with my shield.

Change: neither gives an inch. Toe-to-toe, an exchange of fast, flashing sword-blows, all with exaggeration and flourish, all easy to spot coming. The whole routine. Most of the crowd must have seen it before, but not this fast. Now I'm moving forward again, now he is and I am retreating before a winter-storm of blows. Now me again, locking swords hilt-to-hilt, and grinding them round in a circle – once, twice, again – before springing apart.

As we take a moment to re-appraise the situation, I feel so alive! I have never felt this clear, this clean, this drunk upon afternoon air before. I love life! I love the warmth in my muscles, I love the weight of my shield, I love the roaring in my ears. I have never felt so free since the first time I climbed the tree outside my villa.

We begin again; and again it is a sequence of familiar routines, but now the flourishes are less obvious, the blows are laid on in earnest, and weaknesses are looked for. The crowd's buzz has become a mere murmur, as knowledgeable watchers realise that the real fight has begun.

It is clear now how equally matched we are. Our skills have been sharpened to the same keenness, and no blow can get through. I can anticipate and parry all of

Moloch's jabs and cuts, and can see his feints and changes of direction coming. He has the measure of mine too. Each of us is agile – some big men make the best dancers, the most light of foot, and I have found again, from somewhere, a young girl's grace. I can leap in, attack, and leap away. He can shift from foot to foot, lean one way and then the other to change an attacking angle. We copy each other, almost in sheer mockery of style. Left and right, blows come, fast and heavy, relentless, simultaneous, full of intent and meaning. Killing blows all, notching blade on blade, blade on shield, shield on shield. The air sings with them!

Another change: I am giving ground. I am still parrying and countering all his hardest strokes, and replying with my own, just as hard. I am still easy on my feet, dodging and dancing out of reach. I still have all my strength left. But something is different now. An inequality has surfaced that I now recognise with cold lucidity. We are equally agile. We are equally adept. He is stronger. Slowly, I am being driven back. This can only mean one thing: I am going to die today.

I have seen this before. I now recall that years ago, when I first started coming to the games, I saw a fight between two apparent equals. They went back and forth like this, no one taking the advantage, until there was an almost imperceptible shift in the scene, and it became possible to see that one of them was vulnerable. At that point, the roaring of the crowd had intensified. It does so now.

Many people are calling my name, rallying behind me, urging me on, and indeed I redouble my efforts and regain some ground. But it is only momentary, and now Moloch is pressing forward again. Double cut to my face, taken on the shield, step back and change guard. Barged shield to shield, step back, change guard and give an overarm cut to the head, easily fended off. Step back under a series of alternating slashes with the sword and punches with the shield boss. Counter-attack, no way through. Parry, counter-thrust, no way through, step back, change guard. Duck a backhander, step back from a chop with the shield edge, change guard and thrust, no way through. My sword is forced away by an upward sweep from his shield, step back, change guard and stand my ground, no, step back and parry. Another parry, weaker, step back, change guard. With every backward step my death is closer, and yet, more and more, I am so alive, so in love with life, so eager to live to be a thousand years old!

We lock hilt-to-hilt, and he pushes. Step back, change guard – No! Suddenly there is a mighty thump in my back which winds me. I have collided with the wall! Now my shield is knocked aside, and I am down on one knee. Moloch's sword-arm is back, ready to make a thrust at my breast-bone. Can I sense a moment's hesitation? No matter, because in desperation I push, and spin, and scramble to get out of the way, knowing that he is upon me and will have no hesitation in striking at my naked, unprotected back.

I'm still alive. I have found my way back onto my feet, and I spin around on my toes to face him, looking all about me. Where is he? I stop.

He has not followed me. He is standing a pace back from where he had me at his mercy. His sword is at his side, half-raised, or rather half-lowered. He is dumbly looking at the wall where I had been all but pinned. Then he turns his head, and looks straight at me. I can see only shadow under his visor, but I know his gaze is on my face. The crowd is stunned into silence, as am I, and all of a sudden that vital zest and clarity that I had felt is draining from me. I feel tired, and sick, and I realise that he had let me go. I had been dead, and he had given me life, and now I have no more taste for it. I have barely enough motivation to move quickly to the centre of the arena, and to take up something approaching a fighting stance. He turns, faces me, but does not move, and now the stunned silence of the crowd is peppered with angry catcalls. That brings a kind of reaction from him, and he steps towards me. A few paces only. Still he looks straight at me, but does not raise his guard. What is he doing?

The anger of the crowd is beginning to boil, and now I too am infected by it. I stamp my foot. I kick up a cloud of sand. Anything to break this stand-off.

"You fool! You damned idiot!" I yell. "They'll haul us both out of here and crucify us like a couple of forgers! Do you want that? Fight! Fight for your life! It's what you were bred up to do!"

I put my sword down and fling a handful of sand at him. Then I pick up my sword again, and rush at him, barging him with my shield. He staggers two paces back, steadies, and takes a guard, but does not move.

"Idiot! Idiot! Idiot!" I yell, and the crowd takes up the chant, "Idiot! Idiot! Idiot!"

I dance in again and whack the back of his legs with the flat of my sword. Then I bash his helmet, then his legs again. Suddenly he is attacking once more, charging forward, swinging with both sword and shield. But he is attacking me without skill, blindly, desperately, as if angry at something unseen that hangs in the air between us. His blows miss, go wide, very few fall against my

sword or shield. I am falling back again, but without
effort, still trying to take in what is happening. When I
stand and parry and counter-thrust, I get through, and my
sword-point is turned aside by his armour instead of by
his weapons. Still he comes wildly on, still the crowd is
chanting, but only I can hear the steady keening coming
from under his helmet. The first and only sound I have
ever heard him make, wordless, full of years of pain and
rage, a death-song. I have loved life, he now hates it, and
hates it intensely. The crowd is still chanting, taunting
him, but a few of them start to give the wolf-howl that I
taught them. More and more take it up, and I know now
what they want me to do. I brought them here, I held
them in the palm of my hand for only a brief moment.
Now they hold me.

So I meet, parry, and counter Moloch's wild blows,
making every stroke ring and thunder, sword to sword,
sword to shield, shield to shield. At some point I must
have got through, because his right arm is cut, and there
is another trickle of blood on his right leg. Still he comes
on, that thin wailing issuing from his helmet, blows
battering at me like hail in a cross-wind, making me
fight. Now *I* don't want to do this, and would gladly go
back to the wall, put my back to it, let him kill me. But it
is all out of my hands, and now I too am battering at him

wildly. I have a bruise on my shield-arm, and I am cut somewhere too, but he is cut more badly, and his keening is coming in gasps. I can do nothing more. I can only hammer away at him with all of my strength. He can only hammer back, but his strength, once greater than mine, is now failing. I have hurt him badly. My next blow knocks the sword from his grasp, another severs the straps of his shield, a third forces him to his knees, and he topples over onto one elbow exhausted.

I stand over him as he fiddles with the strap of his helmet, and as he pulls it free, I kick his arm away and he lies flat. Now I kneel, pinning his arm, my sword is at his throat. I have pulled my helmet off too. He is looking at me, but I can't meet his gaze. Instead, I look up at the tribunal, at the small, purple figure standing there. The crowd is looking at him too; they are all making the wolf-howl, but I am no longer the centre of their world, that insignificant purple figure is, as they all make the sign for death. A dramatic pause, and it is confirmed. Death, so longed for, is given.

Now I do meet Moloch's eyes, and I pause. I see such trust, such resignation, such love in them. No one has ever looked at me that way, and a hardness in my throat makes me catch my breath. With my free hand, I caress his cheek.

Then I give the single thrust as much weight as mercy can lend to a tired body. I sever his spine at the neck, and the look in his eyes isn't there any more. Nothing is.

I stand, and though my eyes are stinging with all the tears that I have never cried before, I raise my arms to acknowledge the shouts of the crowd. Some still howl, but others have taken up a new chant.

"*Roma, Lupa! Roma, Lupa!*"

Yes, yes! Oh yes! Rome is the She-wolf! Not the one who suckles the young Romulus and Remus, though. The She-wolf is Rome! The great monster that devours her own children.

"*Roma, Lupa! Roma, Lupa!*"

My name on everyone's lips, and *Infama* becomes *Fama* at last. Because I am Rome, and Rome is me. No freedom from this for me, because I am the city's greatest asset. Why? Because I remind her just what she is, where her *arete* and her *ergon* can be found. Because I devoured my child, and the city devoured me – this is what it will be like for the rest of my life. And I will be immortal. For ever, and ever, and ever..

CHAPTER XVII

Franjo was in the bedroom, lying down. When I checked, he was asleep on top of the bed. He had loosened his tie – Vittorio's tie, naturally – but had kept his shoes on, as if ready to get up and make a run for it at the first alarm. He was, however, completely out for the count. He had looked tired when he walked into the flat; now, asleep, he simply looked vulnerable. As I watched him, from the doorway, I felt I should have been happy, but now there was a kind of bathos in his being here. There was no catharsis, just another problem, and when I caught myself thinking that way about my long-lost and now-found boyfriend, my shoulders slumped, guiltily. Vittorio called me softly from the lounge, and I turned back, leaving the bedroom door slightly open, as though shutting it would somehow make Franjo disappear back over the Adriatic. I came and sat opposite Vittorio, and stared distractedly at the wall.

"What will you do now?" asked Vittorio.

"I don't know. My friends said nothing about using the flat to house a refugee lover. My money is running low. Everything is different. Again."

"And to cap it all you have a crush on a Catholic

priest!" he said, with a smile. "Don't worry, it's quite common here in Italy, and young women tend to get over it. Don't tell me you or your friends never looked at the new Orthodox priest when he arrived at the local Serbian church?"

"Oh, please!" I retorted. "They all have beards, and funny hats too. The last one I met smelled bad. In any case, you infernally arrogant beast! What gives you the right to say things like that, even if they are true? You led me on!" I must have been feeling better now, because I was going after him! He was shaking his head. "Yes you did – don't deny it! You hid who you were, from the very beginning. You could have told me, but you didn't. You let me think you were some sort of professor at first – and then you let me think you were a *Capo Mafioso!*"

Now Vittorio had both eyebrows raised. "That won't do. Jelena, I told you I was a priest during our first conversation in the café. You would not have remembered that, I suppose, because you were so busy staring out of the window, feeling aggrieved at everything. You just didn't listen to me, did you?"

It was more of an accusation than a question, and of course he was right. I had been so wrapped up in myself, in my own feelings, in the turmoil of my busy-busy mind, that I had ignored all the obvious things about him that fitted in with what he was now saying. His old fashioned gallantry and the frustrating way he refused to court me now made sense – being celibate he had to be on his best behaviour, not open to accusations of breaking a vow of chastity. Now I could see why people not only deferred to him, but looked quizzically at me as we went about together. As I was not a Catholic, or even a Christian of any sort – I had made that plain from the beginning – he had never addressed me as he might have addressed an Italian girl. I was always "Jelena" when we talked together, or "Signorina Stepanovic" when he introduced me. I was never "my child", or "daughter". Now I laughed. But it was a fragile laugh, and I didn't know whether I would burst into tears again. I hoped not, but just in case, I tugged Vittorio's handkerchief from his hand.

We said nothing for some time. I became distracted by a pigeon outside the window. Vittorio called me back by speaking my name. He looked at me and said, in a more serious voice than he had ever used to me, "You are probably the most deeply troubled person I have ever met. I did not say disturbed, because that sounds insulting, but nonetheless there is something or there are some things that disturb you, right inside you, right in your heart. I know this. I am right, aren't I?"

"Yes you are. But I really haven't the first idea what half these things which disturb me are, let alone how to organise a defence against them."

"Let's start with the most obvious: your dreams of ancient Rome. They are not real."

"But they are! They are! You would have had to be me to know this. When I think of the jumble of insane impressions that have been my dreams before these. They're so different. Ancient Rome, the barracks, the arena, were all sharp and vivid to me. I remember a whole life, I remember people, sensations, feelings. I remember thinking and speaking in a completely different language. Vittorio, I remember dying!"

He was shaking his head. "Life in ancient Rome was nothing like what you described to me. You made so many errors of fact. There never was a gladiatorial barracks quite like you described. No Jelena..." he held up his hand, and stopped me from interrupting, "... I'm sorry, but it wasn't real. I know it seemed so to you. You have not lived before. You were not Lupa in a previous life. There was no Lupa. Of that I am very sure."

"But I'm sure there was, and that I was her." I was on the edge of my seat now, and almost shouting, so that Vittorio had to shush me, and point to the open door to the room where Franjo slept. I went on in an angry whisper. "Anyhow, if we are talking about things which are and things which are not, you believe that when you pass your hand over a cup of wine and a wafer, and chant some arcane words, they miraculously turn into the actual blood and flesh of Jesus Christ. Don't lecture me about what's real!"

"That's different."

"Why?"

"Because it is the teaching of the Mother Church, and it is the will of God."

"Oh, please!"

Vittorio shrugged his shoulders and smiled. "You see," he went on. "You have the same problem with something that I know to be true, and which you consider to be a delusion at best. How can I prove to you that transubstantiation is something vital, utterly real, a miracle of daily life to a priest? No – to you it's absurd, a physical impossibility, totally against the laws of the universe, and you don't believe in it. So if I tell you that your own experiences are totally at odds with reality too, what then? Where can we go to from here? You will be angry with me if I tell you that they are something to do with your depression, because you are a good communist, with a good, communist mistrust of psychology and psychiatry. What is more, you are a rationalist, and deeply ashamed of how irrational you are when you are depressed. But you are just that – *deeply irrational* – in such states. How do you know that these dreams are not some, well, neurosis?"

My blood was up. "Oh, spare me the pop-psychology! What makes you an expert?"

"Several years of sitting on the other side of a grill from all kinds of human beings, while they pour their hearts out to me. And their minds. That's what. Sometimes I feel more like a sick-bowl or a lavatory!" With that last remark he threw out his arms wide, with a look of almost comic desperation on his face, and I had to burst out laughing.

"Okay," I said, when I had stifled the last giggle. "So where do I go from here? What have you got in the way of penance for me? How many *Paters*? How many *Aves*? What am I going to do about these dreams? What am I going to do about my money running out? What am I going to do about anything? You are so ready with your psych-babble, *Babbo mio*, how about some hard advice for a good communist?"

"I am beginning to see the real Jelena," said Vittorio. "She has always been here, but kept underneath. Let me try to explain it this way. Have you ever seen or heard of the old fortune-telling cards – *i tarrochi* – the major and minor arcana? No? As a priest I am not supposed to set much store by such things, but I have been in rural parishes and urban slums where superstition and the church overlay each other, and where curses and fate are part of everyday life. Anyhow, one card of the major pack is a skeleton wielding a scythe: the death card. When an adept casts someone's life in the cards that card is supposed to mean, superficially of course, that person's death. But it has another meaning, which is an ending, and a sweeping clear of everything that has gone before. So it is often seen as a positive influence. It represents a chance for someone to start with a completely clean slate. Since the death of Lupa your dreams have gone, yes? Lupa has been swept away. Let's say that she was the phoney Jelena, the superficial you. Well, she's gone now, and the real you emerges from her psychic prison."

He paused. His face softened into a look of gentle concern. "You've had it rough for a long time, without realising it. You often told me about how insubstantial things appeared to you – illusions of permanence with nothing but shift, shift, shift underneath. Well, that's come to an end for you. It hurts, like the cauterising of a wound. It's scary, like sudden release after years in prison. But that's exactly what it is. There will be no going back for you. Franjo is alive, but the past is dead. The death card has been turned up, and everything has been swept away. The real you is out in the open, and the future is waiting for her."

I sat in silence for many minutes, taking all this in. I couldn't quite grasp it. Vittorio seemed to be very close to telling me something very important, but even he with his years of experience listening to neurotic, guilt-ridden *signore*, he did not know how.

"Another coffee?" I asked, lamely.

Vittorio waved away the offer. "There's something else you need to know," he said.

CHAPTER XVIII

Over the past days – how many days have passed? – I have become very familiar with the ceiling of my room. I have been ill, as good as immobile, I realise this. I hadn't been feeling good since I murdered Moloch for the good of Rome. Back in the subterranean world of the Flavian amphitheatre, where no member of the audience can see us, someone had handed me a lead cup full of wine sweetened with honey.

I drank it in one gulp, but sicked it up again all over his sandals, and he cursed me.

"Too late," I thought.

Since then I have been able to keep nothing down except bread, and a little water. Yesterday, and the day before, I don't think I ate anything. I hardly speak to anyone. The last conversation I remember, apart from the occasional "I'm all right" when someone asked me how I was feeling, was with one of the servants.

"What's that black stain in the corner of the ceiling?" I asked.

"What black stain? I can't see any black stain."

"Over there. See? In that corner. It has a couple of sharp points. It seems to be growing out of the shadows where the two walls meet." That was the darkest corner of my room, and indeed it was difficult to see where the shadows ended and the stain began. The servant shrugged. He could see nothing, and obviously thought I was mad or delirious. Neither, in fact, was the case. Neither is the case. The darkness – shadow or stain – is still there. It has grown since I first noticed it, and is growing still.

People have come and gone as I have lain here. I once heard a whispered conversation in the corridor.

"They say she's been poisoned. Deliberately! It's the price of fame sometimes – if they can't get you killed off in the arena, they can find other ways."

"Shut up! Do you want her to hear?"

It was nonsense anyway. I haven't been poisoned – not in that sense. In another sense I have. A poison entered me, through my lungs, in the fetid air of the Mithraeum. It has simply taken its time to get a real hold, waiting until I had offered to the soldier's god a mockery of a sacrifice, and killed a wretched innocent. I know why that blackness has spread across my room, what its nature is, if not its very name. I do not think that my illness is one of the body, although it is my body which is virtually paralysed, wasted. Neither is it all in my mind. I am not mad, in fact I see with complete clarity, even though I drift in and out of seeing, and do not know whether I am awake or dreaming.

Wakefulness and dreams are one and the same thing, and I see both clearly. I know I do, despite the pity I have come to recognise in the face of anyone who comes into the room.

At one time there was a familiar face. I wanted it to be Patricius, and for a moment I thought it was. But it melted into the familiar features of the Lanista. What had me fooled for a moment was the softness in his expression. I had never seen that in him. He came and sat by my bed, and spent a long time watching me. Watching over me. I think he even held my hand, though surely that is an unlikely thing for him to have done – perhaps that was someone else. Once he did call for a servant – his secretary – and issued an order. The servant came back with a familiar tablet.

"Do you recognise this? It's your contract. I'm revoking it. See?" He broke it in half. "I can't get you a wooden sword, but at least I can do this for you. You're going to die a free woman – do you understand? No more Lupa. Take back your real name, or take another one if you wish. You're released, discharged, with as much honour as I can give to you."

I think I squeezed his hand, but as it was unlikely that

he was holding it, that must have been someone else's, some other time. But Lupa will be my name forever, despite the Lanista's wish. I can't escape myself that easily. Freedom will not come with the breaking in half of a tablet. I am a slave to something more implacable than him, greater and more terrible than Rome, something immortal, something outside the world that you can touch and feel. This greater thing does not give up its slaves, it does not rip up its contracts, it gives no honourable discharge, it recognises no wooden sword. There comes a time when propitiation no longer works, however, and it tosses you aside, to be disposed of. Nemesis, doom of all who pass into the sunlight and into the gaze of the crowd – at last even Nemesis accepts that the Fates spin, measure out, and cut the thread of a human life where it must be cut. And then you are in hands beyond those of Nemesis.

The ceiling of my room is nearly all shadow now. Just a patch of red remains, which may be torchlight shining through the door, which has remained open all this time, or it may be a reflection of sunset through the window. The shadow itself is solid black, still with two sharp points thrusting into the patch of red. The red is becoming deeper, as the sun is going down.

Perhaps if I climb the tree again, perhaps if I get

higher up, I can make the last vestige of the sun – the red patch of sky – stay a little longer. Then my mother and father will come with a ladder and get me down, and take me to lie on my own bed. My eyes are fixed on that diminishing, dimming patch of red, on the sharp and clear division where the two points jag into it, like two horns. Or like the upright ears of a jackal.

CHAPTER XIX

"What? No! That's just not possible! I don't believe it!" How many different ways are there of denying something? I think I shouted out every single one. I forgot Franjo was sleeping in the next room. I stood over Vittorio, my fists clenched into angry, white balls. This was the last straw, the absolute limit, after everything else that had happened. I could take the total switch-about of Vittorio's identity, I could take the reappearance in my life of Franjo, I could take the possibility that my dreams had been just so much nonsense produced by the subconscious of a depressive – but this I could not take. This I would not take. Denial, denial, denial. I just had to be left with something. There had to be one thing that the death card did not sweep away.

Vittorio shrugged, looking smaller and weaker than he ever had done, as he sat there in his black robes.

"What can I say? It's true, I'm afraid. The silver medallion is a fake."

I sat down hard on the nearest armchair.

"I held it in my hand. I felt it – as near as makes no difference, through latex. It was solid, it was real. It was old. Oh Vittorio, it was real – it *is* real! It was the most wonderful thing I had ever held. Even with its residue of dirt, even with the worn design, it was so – oh, how can I put this – it was downright radioactive!" Now I was talking nonsense.

"Look," said Vittorio. "Yes, it's old, I'll grant you. But I had my doubts about it from the beginning, and I should have said something more openly. That's what all the discussions with Signor Ciani were about. That's why it had to be sent away. It turns out that it's Renaissance, not Roman. Now there's a scandal about it. Some people are saying that the site is not Roman at all – we know it is, but the facts don't stop a good story amongst the ignorant. But in any case, there's the further scandal generated by the puzzle of who put it there and when. And why. Could someone simply have dropped it down a rabbit hole in fifteen-hundred-and-something? Improbable. So someone must have obtained it recently, and placed it where it would be found. Who? Some say me. Some say Signor Ciani. Some say one of the other workers. Some say it was the developer's men, hoping to discredit the dig. Well if it was the latter, they've succeeded! Our work has been called off, and the bulldozers will roll six weeks ahead of schedule."

"But why is anyone saying it was you?"

He shrugged again. "Jelena, I must confess – hah! – that I'm in trouble. Even someone of my rank can get in trouble. This mess happens on a dig which is under my oversight, and it happens when I am off on an unauthorised trip to Croatia, on an ill-defined mission, interfering with the priests of a separate diocese. I'm back in Italy with someone who is, to all intents and purposes, an illegal immigrant. On top of that, I have been seen all around the city, in mufti, with a young woman!"

I must admit that I hadn't thought about that. I had got him into trouble. All the inconvenience I had put him through, all the bad things I had thought about him, all the flirting that I thought I had done so subtly! And all the time he was simply a generous, caring man, who had risked his reputation to do good by stealth.

"One thing I don't really understand is how come you were in charge of the dig in the first place?" I said, trying to change the direction of the conversation a little, away from our personal embarrassment.

"That's easy. The land belongs to the Church. Or it does until the bulldozers move in."

There was another silence. I stared at the last centimetre of coffee, cold, in my mug, and at the *biscotti* crumbs on the coffee table.

"You asked me what I was going to do now," I said at last. "I have no answer for that question. I haven't the faintest idea what I *can* do. I have all these questions buzzing around my head. The dreams have stopped, but what were they? You say you don't believe they were anything real, and that there are so many things you can't square with what you know of life in Rome back then. But they were so completely vivid. What can I do with the story those dreams told me? Then there's Franjo. I have to sort out precisely how I feel about him after all this time apart. We are now different people, and what we feel about each other is, I think, still stuck in pre-war Srebrenice. Could we go back there as a couple, a Serb wife and a Croat husband, now that I am a success in Italy – or I was until I fell off my horse – and live quietly, or become activists for reconciliation? I doubt it. Peace is only skin deep in the Balkans. Smiles show teeth. I have to sort out how I feel about you too, you know. You have turned me on my head, and you can't deny it. You're a good man, Vittorio, but you must admit you were to some extent playing a little game with me. I know – let's run away together, and watch the newspapers headlines from a safe distance: Playboy Priest Elopes with Bareback Lover! I am joking, I really am – don't look so horrified! Oh, I could get on a plane for Australia if it comes to that. I wish I had the medallion, somehow, with its bitter inscription about this city. It seems to be a thing which decides a course for someone. I could toss it in the air and see what side faces up when it lands. I could do that with a Euro, though!"

At that point, Vittorio took on a new role – that of a prophet.

"You could write a book," he said. "No, I mean it. And if the dreams start to get away from you, so what? That might be for the best. Look at it this way: people have come to me, have sat the other side of a little partition and told me things about themselves, sometimes with deep shame, sometimes with grudging resignation, but always with a sense that they have sinned and must tell me about it. I listened to them, told them that they were forgiven. The Hail Marys and Our Fathers I gave them to repeat had little bearing on what they had done or what they had told me. These things are a kind of catharsis in their own right. The fact that they were already contrite was enough to save them."

"Sounds dangerously like Protestantism to me... Don Vittorio" I said.

Vittorio waved a hand as though he were impatient with me. "There's little difference between Catholic and Protestant. Catholicism teaches that a person is saved by faith and by good works, Protestantism says by faith alone but the good works follow. The effect is the same, the good works get done. If you like I'll say *ego te absolvo* right now and writing the book can be your penance. What actually comes out in the end doesn't matter. Your freedom does. Your 'sin' of dreaming will have gone away."

Could I write a book? It might be fun to have me and Franjo brought together, with a "Reader, I married him". Or even more fun to involve Vittorio at the end, with "Reader, he married us"! Oh, I don't know, I really don't know. If I did write a best-seller, the money it would bring in might – just *might* – help stave off the inexorable journey to the next milestone of impermanence, and the one after that.

Many things in life are fakes. The old Chinese proverb, "May you live in interesting times", is a fake. It doesn't stop times being interesting, though, and these surely are. And it doesn't stop living in them being tantamount to living under a curse. A silver medallion may be a fake, but it can still exert a magnetic tug one way or the other. A self-image can be the biggest fake of all. Here's something, a piece of Latin verse I found on the internet – I had an idea what it meant, but Vittorio gave me a good, free translation:

Here are the girls who blow fanfares to Flora.

Or maybe they have more profound plans, and are getting themselves ready

For the arena itself! How can a woman still be decent

If she stuffs her head in a helmet, denying the sex she was born with?

They adore virile exploits, but they wouldn't want actually to be men.

Poor, weak things – they think – how little they really enjoy it!

What a great honour it is for a husband to see, at an auction,

Where his wife's property is up for sale, belts, greaves,

Arm-guards, and helmet-plumes!

Hear her grunt and groan as she works out – parrying and thrusting.

See her neck bent down under the weight of the helmet.

Look at the rolls of bandage and tape, making her legs like tree-trunks.

Then have a laugh after the practice session is over, to see her,

Armour and weapons put aside, squatting on the pot!

You decadent girls – descended from praetors and consuls –

Tell us, whom have you seen in such a get-up,

Panting and sweating like this? No gladiator's bit on the side,

No hard-bitten stripper would even try!

Was that really me in another life? I don't know any more. But old Nemesis, that's a different matter. I'm beginning to believe in that old, pagan deity. Isn't there something outside ourselves which makes us fatalistic, as we get tossed around, or makes us superstitious enough to turn over our money at every new moon? Sometimes we incline one way with a shrug of the shoulders, sometimes we incline the other with a set jaw and a straight back. The only thing that is certain, from all that, is that we human beings are a race of contortionists. I wish I knew whether the proverb about a journey of a thousand miles beginning with a single step is a fake too, then I might really set off somewhere with a purpose in mind.

But right now Vittorio has gone, Franjo is still sleeping – I just looked in on him – and I am staring out of the window at the familiar view, the scene which was so flat and unreal that time when Vittorio found me curled up on the floor. There has been a rain shower and now there is sun. That must mean something. If the City truly is a monster then there are times when its scales – its lamellar armour – shine and make it seem beautiful.

*

~ Lupa ~

MARIE MARSHALL is a poet, writer and blogger who is well recognized for her poetry online and in literary circles.

A collection of poems, "Naked in the Sea", was published in 2010 and can be purchased off the internet from Masque Publishing.

Marie's website: http://mairibheag.com.